PENGUIN BOOKS

THE DIG

'Superbly crafted, delightful . . . to be treasured'
Sunday Telegraph

'A rich vein of dry humour runs throughout' *Evening Standard*

'Beautifully written . . . there is a true and wonderful ending to the
story' Bill Wyman, *Mail on Sunday*

'Wistful and poignant. A masterpiece in Chekhovian
understatement' *The Times Literary Supplement*

'A delicate, quietly affecting human drama' *Daily Mail*

'A moving novel that coheres wonderfully as it progresses' *Spectator*

'A delicate evocation of a vanished era' *Sunday Times*

The Dig

john preston

PENGUIN BOOKS

PENGUIN BOOKS

Published by the Penguin Group
Penguin Books Ltd, 80 Strand, London WC2R 0RL, England
Penguin Group (USA) Inc., 375 Hudson Street, New York, New York 10014, USA
Penguin Group (Canada), 90 Eglinton Avenue East, Suite 700, Toronto, Ontario, Canada M4P 2Y3
(a division of Pearson Penguin Canada Inc.)
Penguin Ireland, 25 St Stephen's Green, Dublin 2, Ireland (a division of Penguin Books Ltd)
Penguin Group (Australia), 707 Collins Street, Melbourne, Victoria 3008, Australia
(a division of Pearson Australia Group Pty Ltd)
Penguin Books India Pvt Ltd, 11 Community Centre, Panchsheel Park, New Delhi – 110 017, India
Penguin Group (NZ), 67 Apollo Drive, Rosedale, Auckland 0632, New Zealand
(a division of Pearson New Zealand Ltd)
Penguin Books (South Africa) (Pty) Ltd, Block D, Rosebank Office Park,
181 Jan Smuts Avenue, Parktown North, Gauteng 2193, South Africa

Penguin Books Ltd, Registered Offices: 80 Strand, London WC2R 0RL, England

www.penguin.com

First published by Viking 2007
Published in Penguin Books 2008

018

Copyright © John Preston, 2007
All rights reserved.

The moral right of the author has been asserted

Typeset by Rowland Phototypesetting Ltd, Bury St Edmunds, Suffolk
Printed and bound in Great Britain by Clays Ltd, Elcograf S.p.A.

ISBN: 978-0-141-01638-2

www.greenpenguin.co.uk

To Susanna and Joseph

Prologue

That evening I came back and worked on alone. The rectangle of darkened earth at the entrance to the burial chamber showed up quite clearly in front of me. I scraped away with the trowel and then I switched to the bodkin. It wasn't long after starting that I came across this greenish band. It was running through the soil like a grass stain. At first, I thought my eyes were playing up. I had to blink a few times before I'd allow myself to believe it.

With the pastry brush, I swept the earth away, taking off as much as I dared. I was worried that if I took any more away the whole thing might vanish completely. But far from disappearing, the green band showed up even more distinctly than before.

Then, to the left of the first one, I found another green band. The colour was a little duller than before – more speckled too – but still impossible to miss. I took these to be the remains of bronze hoops. Possibly belonging to a barrel, or some sort of wooden container.

When I looked at my watch, I saw that it had already gone nine o'clock. I was astonished – I thought I'd been going for about fifteen minutes. The light was fading now.

Even so, I was in a muck sweat. I kept having to wipe my forehead with my sleeve. I knew I was going to have to give up soon. But I couldn't bear to stop. Not yet.

I kept on brushing. More than anything else I wished I'd brought a torch and I cursed myself for not thinking of it before. Just when I had decided that there was no point carrying on, I came across something else. A piece of timber.

To begin with, I assumed this must be the barrel, or what was left of the barrel. It wasn't long, though, before I had second thoughts. The piece of timber was about the size of a large book. Like a ledger, or a church Bible. As far as I could tell, it was perfectly flat. In places, it was so decayed that even my pastry brush was too rough. All I could do was put my lips as close as possible and blow the earth away.

In one place, though, it was quite solid. When I tapped the wood with my finger, it gave out a soft, hollow sound. In the top left-hand corner, I could make out what I thought was a knot. Peering at it more closely, I saw it was a small hole. A dry, papery smell rose from the ground. It caught in my nostrils as I sat staring at the piece of wood, and at the hole in particular.

Then I did something shameful. Something I can never excuse, or properly explain. I pushed my finger through the hole. It went in quite easily – the timber fitted snugly round my knuckle. Beyond was a cavity. Although I couldn't be sure, I felt the cavity to be a large one. There was a kind of emptiness around my finger, like an absence of air.

I stayed where I was for several minutes. By now I could hardly see the wood in front of me, it was so dark. But still I sat there, not moving. And when at last I took my finger

2

away, all the excitement I'd felt before vanished in an instant. In its place came a great wash of sadness. So strong it quite knocked me back.

After I'd covered over the centre of the ship with tarpaulins and secured the corners with stones, I set off for Sutton Hoo House. The gravel path ran pale and straight in front of me. On one side was a yew tree. I could see its silhouette looming up before me, its branches almost touching the ground. The sky was black as hogs.

When I rang the back doorbell, I could feel the sweat, cold and drying, on my skin. Grateley answered the door. Although he'd taken off his collar, he still had his tail coat on.

'Basil? What are you doing here?'

'Would you tell Mrs Pretty I need to see her?' I told him.

'Now?' He swayed back in surprise. 'Do you know what time it is? Mrs Pretty will be preparing for bed.'

'Even so, I need to see her.'

Behind him, light bounced off the white tiles. Grateley gave me a look. Frowning mostly, although there might have been some sympathy in it.

'I'm sorry, Basil,' he said. 'You'll just have to wait until morning.'

Edith Pretty
April–May 1939

There was a knock on the door.

'Come in.'

'Mr Brown, ma'am,' said Grateley, and then stood aside to let him in.

I am not sure quite what I had been expecting, but it was not this. My first impression was that everything about him was brown – dark brown. His skin was mahogany-coloured. So were his clothes: a cotton tie, a tweed jacket with the top button fastened and what appeared to be a cardigan beneath. He was like a kipper in human form. It seemed absurd that his name should be Brown too.

The only things about him that were not brown were his eyes. Grey, like two polished tacks, they gleamed with alertness. His hair stood up in tufts. He was holding an object in his left hand – brown, inevitably – mashed between his fingers. The other was jutting out in front of him.

'Mrs Pretty,' he said.

'It was good of you to come, Mr Brown.'

'No, no, no . . .'

His handshake was dry and firm.

'Won't you sit down?' I indicated the sofa.

He did so, but only just, perching on the edge of the seat with his elbows on his knees. The brown object was still in his hand. My gaze was drawn to it. I thought – I am afraid I thought it might be an animal of some sort. Then I realized it was his cap. He must have seen me looking, because he unclenched his hand, placing the cap on the cushion beside him.

'Mr Brown, you have been recommended to me as someone who knows about soil. Suffolk soil. Mr Reid Moir, the chairman of Ipswich Museum Committee, spoke highly of you.'

He twisted slightly at the mention of Reid Moir, I thought, but nothing more than that. I remembered how Reid Moir had described him as being somewhat unorthodox in his methods. I remembered too how he had also referred to him as a local man, laying a good deal of stress on the word 'local'. At the time his meaning had passed me by, but now I saw it clearly enough.

'As you may know,' I went on, 'I have a number of mounds on my land. I have been thinking for some time of having them excavated. Mr Reid Moir told me that you might be the man for the job.'

There was no reaction – not at first. Then he said, 'What do you think might be in your mounds, Mrs Pretty?'

His accent was broad Suffolk, with scarcely any vowels coming through and the consonants all clattering into one another.

'I am assuming they are prehistoric. Probably Bronze Age. As for what, if anything, may be inside, I would not care to speculate. From what I can tell, they do not appear to have been excavated before. It is rumoured that Henry VII dug for treasure in a mound here. We also know that John Dee, Elizabeth I's Court Astrologer, was commissioned to search for treasure along this stretch of coast. Some people say he came here too, although there is no evidence of his having done so.'

Again he said nothing. Despite his clothes, there was something oddly spruce about him. Possibly it was his air of containment.

'Would you care to have a look for yourself?' I suggested.

Outside, the landscape was drained of colour. The water in the estuary looked hard and shiny. It might not have been moving at all. Underfoot, the grass was spongy and already damp with dew. I was careful where to put my feet. Mr Brown walked with his arms bowed and his elbows sticking out, as if his jacket was too small.

'This whole area around Sutton Hoo House has always been known as Little Egypt,' I told him. 'No doubt on account of the mounds. There are a number of legends about them. People claim to have seen mysterious figures dancing in the moonlight. Even a white horse. I believe that local girls used to lie down on top of them in the hope of becoming pregnant.'

Mr Brown glanced across at me, his eyebrows rising in two perfectly inverted Vs. 'And have you ever seen any of these dancing figures yourself, Mrs Pretty?' he asked.

'No,' I said, laughing. 'Never.'

A coverlet of mist was clinging to the mounds. When we came closer to the largest of them, Mr Brown made a little clicking sound with his tongue. 'They're bigger than I expected. Much bigger.'

He pointed upwards. 'May I?'

'By all means.'

He ran up the side of the mound, elbows pumping away. When he reached the top, he stood looking round. Then he promptly disappeared. After a few seconds, I realized that he must have knelt down behind a clump of bracken. Then he straightened up and stamped on the ground – first with one foot, then the other. He stayed up on the mound for several more minutes. When he came back down he was shaking his head.

'What is it, Mr Brown?'

'You have rabbits, Mrs Pretty.'

'Yes, I am aware of that.'

'Rabbits burrow,' he said. 'They're bad for excavations. Very bad. They disturb the soil.'

'Ah, I didn't realize.'

'Oh yes, a real menace, rabbits are.'

After that we went round each mound in turn. Mr Brown paced out measurements, making notes with a stub of pencil in an old diary. At one point a flock of geese went overhead, their necks extended, their wings thumping the air. As he lifted his head to follow them, I saw the sharpness of his profile against the sky.

By the time we had finished the dusk was thickening. Boats were still coming back up the river to Woodbridge, their lanterns lit and their motors chugging. On the slipway, voices were shouting to one another, although only these shreds of sound were audible, not the words.

Back in the sitting room, his hand reached for his jacket pocket. Then it stopped short, hovering above the flap.

'Do feel free to smoke, Mr Brown.'

'It's a pipe,' he said by way of warning.

'That's all right. I don't mind a pipe.'

He took the pipe out of his pocket, along with a pouch

of tobacco. Once he had filled the bowl he lit the tobacco, then pushed it down with his thumb – the tip was completely black. A low, bubbling sound emerged from the interior of the pipe. When he sucked on it, something extraordinary happened: his entire face collapsed. The insides of his cheeks must have almost touched in the middle. When he exhaled, his face inflated again.

'Be a big job,' he said, shaking out the match.

'I could let you have one man,' I said, thinking of John Jacobs, the under-gardener. 'Possibly two.'

'Two would be better. And scuppits.'

'Scuppits?'

'Shovels.'

'I think we could probably run to shovels.'

A cloud of blue smoke rose and settled above his head. 'Mrs Pretty,' he said, 'I must be frank with you. These mounds of yours have almost certainly been robbed. Most of the ones around here were emptied in the seventeenth century. I wouldn't want you getting your hopes up.'

'But would you be willing to try?'

'Yes,' he said. 'Yes, I would . . . That's assuming the details could be agreed.'

'The details, of course. You could lodge with the Lyonses. Mr Lyons is my chauffeur and Mrs Lyons is in charge of the kitchen. There is a spare bedroom in their quarters above the garage. As for money, would one pound, twelve shillings and sixpence a week be acceptable?'

He nodded, almost brusquely.

'I will arrange for you to be paid each week through the cashier at Footman Pretty's store in Ipswich. Should you need money for incidental expenses, please let me know. If I am not here my butler, Mr Grateley, can always pass on any messages. Now then, how long do you think you will need?'

'Four or five weeks should do it. Six at a push.'

'That long?'

'I'll go as fast as I can, Mrs Pretty. But you can't rush something like this.'

'No, I understand. My only concern is that we might not have that much time.'

'Best not hang about, then.'

'No, indeed. When do you think you could start? Would next Monday be too soon?'

'I don't believe it would, no.'

The door burst open and Robert ran in. He came towards my chair, then stopped in the middle of the carpet.

'Ugh! What's that disgusting smell, Mama? Has the silage caught fire again?'

'Robbie,' I said, 'this is Mr Brown.'

Mr Brown had stood up. His head came through the smoke cloud.

'This is my son, Robert,' I said, standing up myself.

I could sense Mr Brown's surprise as his eyes went back and forth, from one of us to the other. A flicker of puzzlement before propriety took over.

'Hello there, young man.'

Robert said nothing; he just kept staring up at him.

'Mr Brown is an archaeologist,' I explained. 'He is going to have a look inside the mounds.'

Robert turned back to face me.

'Inside the mounds? What for?'

My hands were on his shoulders. As he moved, I could feel the bones shifting beneath his skin.

'For treasure,' I said.

*

In Monday's newspaper there was an advertisement below the Invalids column for something called tinned bread:

In response to widespread trade and public demand, the Ryvita company announces that their world-famous crispbread is being supplied in specially sealed tins – both airtight and gas-proof. The wholemeal nourishing form of daily bread, which is so highly commended by doctors and dentists, makes it an ideal item for emergency food storage.

As I was reading this, a movement caught my eye. I looked across the table and saw Robert struggling to eat his egg and bacon. The knife and fork looked enormous in his hands, great eating irons that seemed about to overbalance at any moment.

'Are you sure you can manage, darling?'

He carried on eating, too intent on what he was doing to reply. When he had finished, he put his knife and fork side by side before drawing the napkin carefully across his mouth. Afterwards, he peered at the napkin, drawing one edge between his fingers and inspecting the smear of egg yolk left on it.

'Please may I get down now?' he asked.

'If you are quite sure that you have finished.'

When he nodded, the underside of his chin was as white as the plate.

'What are you going to do this morning?'

He hesitated, then said, 'I thought I would see if Mr Brown was here.'

'Robbie, you're not to get in Mr Brown's way. Do you understand?'

11

'But, Mama, can't I just watch him?' His voice had risen and stretched.

'Later on you can. Later . . . This morning, however, I think you should leave him alone. Why don't you go back upstairs and play with your trains? I could ask Mr Lyons if he would like to join you.'

'I don't want to play with Mr Lyons – not again.'

'Now, Robbie, please. Don't whine. What have I told you?'

'When is Miss Price coming back?'

'You already know the answer to that, darling. Miss Price is not coming back until the end of next week.'

Climbing down from his chair, Robert walked slowly and theatrically away from the table with his head bowed and his shoulders slumped. A few moments after he had gone, Grateley came in through the swing door, trailing one leg behind him to make sure that the door did not bang shut. I moved the newspaper so that he could take my plate away.

'Is Mr Brown here yet?' I asked.

'He has been here since seven o'clock, ma'am.'

'Since seven?' I said in surprise.

'Yes, ma'am. However, I asked him to wait until you had finished your breakfast.'

Mr Brown was standing on the back doorstep. He appeared to be wearing the same clothes as before. I apologized for keeping him waiting, but even as I did so I had the sense that I could have been several hours and he would still have been there, waiting patiently. It was a fine morning; the sun was already starting to break through the clouds. Once again, we made our way out to the mounds. However, this time I said that I wished to make a detour via the squash court.

From there I collected the probing iron. Five feet long

and pointed at one end, the iron is similar in size and shape
to a spear, albeit with a hooped handle at one end. Mr
Brown offered to carry it, but I told him I could manage
quite well on my own. Plainly intrigued, he darted inquiring
glances in my direction as we walked along. However, I did
not enlighten him as to my purpose.

Rabbits ran for cover at our approach. There must have
been hundreds of them, a mass of white tails bounding
unhurriedly through the long grass and disappearing into
Top Hat Wood. My gamekeeper, William Spooner, shoots
as many as he can and gives them to Mr Trim, the butcher
in Woodbridge. But now Mr Trim has said he cannot take
any more. Apparently there is no longer the demand. He
suggested we send them to the local kennels instead.

'Have you given any thought to which one you would
like me to attack first, Mrs Pretty?' Mr Brown asked.

'Yes, I have,' I said, and indicated the largest mound. It
was the one he had run up before.

Mr Brown looked at me. Then he shook his head
fractionally from side to side.

'I wouldn't advise that, Mrs Pretty. Not personally
speaking.'

'You would not?'

'No,' he said. 'No, I wouldn't.'

'Why is that?'

'Because it's all hobbly up the top, with a dip in the
middle. That's usually a sign that a mound has been
robbed. In the eighteenth century, thieves used to sink
shafts into the tops of the mounds – "robbers' flutes",
they're known as – and hope to strike lucky in the middle.
You might be better off with one of the smaller ones. Be
quicker. Cheaper too,' he added.

'Which one would you advise, then, Mr Brown?'

He walked over to the smallest mound of all. It was no more than five feet high, although crowned with an unusually thick clump of bracken. He patted the side of it with the flat of his hand.

'I could try this one.'

I needed a few moments to think through the implications of what Mr Brown was suggesting. I had always assumed that we would start with the largest one. It was what Frank and I had always discussed. It was what we had set our hearts on.

'As you wish,' I said. 'However, there is something I would like you to do first.'

I held out the probing iron towards him. 'Would you mind pushing this into the mound, to see if you hit anything?'

He made an admirable job of concealing his surprise; his eyebrows hardly moved. All he said was, 'From the top, Mrs Pretty?'

'Please.'

He ran up the side of the mound. Standing at the centre, he raised his hands over his head and plunged the probing iron into the ground. For the first three feet or so, it went in quite easily, then there was a muffled thud and Mr Brown could go no further. He tried again, his face set even more determinedly than before. But again he hit the same obstruction.

'There's something in there,' he said when he came back down. 'No telling what, of course. But there's something, all right.'

When his breathing had slowed, he examined the probing iron more closely. 'I've never seen one of these before.'

'My late husband had the blacksmith in Bromeswell make it,' I told him. 'To his own design.'

'To his own design?' repeated Mr Brown, still turning the iron over in his hands. 'Is that so?'

I could hear voices coming closer. Spooner and John Jacobs were walking towards us. Jacobs is a thick-set man with sprigs of grey whisker on his cheek. Spooner is a younger man with carefully tended black hair and a large beard. He seems rather shy, although my maid, Ellen, tells me that the local girls think very highly of him. I introduced the two men to Mr Brown. After shaking hands, they stood about uncertainly, not saying anything. Aware that my presence was proving inhibiting, I left them to make a start.

I was quite wrong about Mr Brown. He is not a kipper; he is a terrier. When I walked out to the mounds that afternoon, I saw a great spray of soil being thrown up into the air. The bracken had been cleared and a wedge-shaped gash cut in the side of the mound. There was something shocking and strangely moving about the sight, with the grass pulled away and the damp earth exposed. The mound looked naked, even violated.

In order that the men should have somewhere for their tea, I had suggested they use the shepherd's hut – a corrugated-iron structure on wheels normally kept in the kitchen garden and used for storing tools. This hut had already been hauled across to a patch of flat ground by the edge of the trees. Seeing it in a new setting, I realized how decrepit it was. The sides, in particular, did not seem to be properly fixed to the frame.

The remains of a fire was smoking alongside. As I came closer, I could smell the sweet, resinous smoke of fir cones.

Jacobs and Spooner were leaning on their shovels, talking to one another. They stopped talking as soon as they saw me. The three of us stood in a line as earth continued to fly between Mr Brown's legs – some, but by no means all of it, landing in a wheelbarrow that had been placed behind him.

Once the barrow was full, Jacobs wheeled it over to the edge of the wood and tipped out the contents on to an already substantial pile. The earth was to be kept in one place so that the mound could be restored to its original shape once the excavation was completed.

Mr Brown carried on digging for several more minutes, oblivious to anything else. When he straightened up, his knees were shiny. Pieces of mud remained stuck to his cap.

'I just wanted to make sure you had everything you needed,' I said.

'We're fine, thank you, Mrs Pretty. Aren't we, lads?'

Spooner and Jacobs both grinned. I could see they were as transfixed by Mr Brown as Robert had been. No sooner had this thought crossed my mind than Robert himself came down the steps of the shepherd's hut. He was swinging a piece of bamboo from side to side and would not meet my eye.

'There you are, Robbie.'

'I haven't been here long, Mama,' he said abruptly. 'Anyway, Mr Brown has been telling me things.'

'What has he been telling you?'

'Well, for instance, do you know what the most important part of an archaeologist's body is?'

'No,' I said, 'I don't believe I do.'

'His nose. Isn't that right, Mr Brown?'

Mr Brown started laughing. So too, after a brief pause, did Jacobs and Spooner.

'I don't want you being a nuisance, Robbie.'

'Oh, he's no trouble at all,' said Mr Brown. 'Been giving us a hand, haven't you, young man?'

Robert flushed with pride and embarrassment. 'Mr Brown says you have to smell things out. Also he has been explaining what he has been doing. First he cuts a trench right through the mound. And then he digs down. That's in case there's a pit underneath.'

'And is your nose telling you anything so far, Mr Brown?' I asked.

Bending forward, he picked up a handful of earth and rubbed it between his fingers. 'See how it's all loose? Foamy, even? That's the backfill from the original digging – a mixture of sand and soil. I'm going in horizontally to begin with. Then I'll go down to the original level – just like Master Robert said. That could be anything from two to eight feet below the surface. I'll be able to tell once I've reached it, as the soil will be a different colour. Darker, probably, on account of the ground having never been disturbed. That's where I hope to find any burial chamber. It should show up as a rectangle of lighter soil, just like a trapdoor.'

'Can you tell if the mound has already been robbed?'

He shook his head. 'Much too early to say. Mind you, we've already found something.'

He walked over to where a long grey object lay on the grass and aimed a kick at it with his boot.

'What is that?'

'That's a stone, Mrs Pretty. It must be what I hit with your – your instrument. It's a start, I suppose, but let's hope we can do a little better than that, eh?'

I started to walk back to the house. When I glanced over

my shoulder, I could see no sign of Mr Brown. He must have resumed digging. There was only the glint of his shovel blade and a dark smudge of soil hanging in the air.

At seven o'clock I went upstairs to change for dinner. Ellen was waiting in my bedroom. She is a big-boned girl with unusually pale fingers, the result, presumably, of poor circulation. In the winter she suffers from chilblains. When she started working for me two years ago, I was concerned that she might be clumsy. In fact, she has turned out to be far more attentive and nimble than I ever expected. My only criticism is that she has recently taken to wearing a particularly invasive scent which manages to be sharp and cloying at the same time.

She was standing beside the open cupboard. Rows of dresses were hanging inside, most of them still in their muslin dust-covers.

'What would you like to wear tonight, ma'am?'

I pointed at one of the dresses that was not in a cover. There seemed no point going to any more trouble than necessary.

'The green silk again, ma'am? That's an old favourite, that one, isn't it?'

As she was helping me to put the dress on, Ellen chattered away about members of the staff and what they had been up to. To begin with, I also feared that I might find her talkativeness trying. Instead, I have rather come to enjoy our conversations, even to look forward to them. Apart from anything else, I learn far more about the household from Ellen than I ever could on my own. Although she is not a gossip, she has a natural curiosity about people, as well as a keen ear for their idiosyncrasies.

On the subject of her own circumstances, however, she is rather less forthcoming. For several months she was stepping out with a boy from Woodbridge. However, it has been some weeks now since she last mentioned him and so I suspect this is no longer the case.

Once we had finished, she asked if I wanted her to repin my hair. I said that would not be necessary.

'I could just give it a quick comb if you like, ma'am.'

'No, thank you, my dear.'

I wonder if Ellen has noticed that I am losing my hair. She can scarcely have failed to do so. But while she may be something of a chatterbox, there is a natural discretion about her too. It is another of her virtues.

At eight o'clock, Grateley knocked on the swing door that leads out from the dining room to the kitchen. For such a bony man, it never ceases to surprise me that he should have such a cushioned-sounding knock. It is as if he has little pillows on each of his knuckles. Silently, he brought the tureen into the dining room and carried it over to the table.

After Grateley had ladled out the soup, he asked me if I wanted to listen to the news. In anticipation of my saying yes, he had already moved over to the sideboard and was about to lift the lid of the wireless. However, I had no desire to listen to the news; it was certain to be alarming or depressing, or quite possibly both. Instead, I told him that tonight I would rather read.

When he had gone, I opened my copy of Howard Carter's account of the excavation of the tomb of Tutankhamun and propped it against the tureen. Increasingly, I have found myself reading about the past. It is a retreat, of course. I know that. None the less, there is something peculiarly comforting in reading about events that have already happened. This as opposed to those that seem to hang, half-formed, above one's head.

Once again I read Carter's description of the discovery of the king's burial chamber:

For the moment, time as a factor in human life has lost its meaning. Three thousand, four thousand years maybe, have passed and gone since human feet last trod the floor on which you stand, and yet, as you note the signs of recent life around you – the half-filled bowl of mortar for the door, the blackened lamp, the finger-mark upon the freshly painted surface, the farewell garland dropped upon the threshold – you feel it might have been but yesterday.

Grateley brought in the main course: boiled beef with carrots. The smell rose from the plate. As it did so, my gorge rose with it. Partly to put off having to start eating, I asked after Grateley's wife – she works as a nurse at the cottage hospital.

'She's quite well, thank you, ma'am.'

'And you, Grateley, how are you?'

'I too am quite well,' he allowed.

'Is your lumbago any better?'

'Still playing up a little, ma'am. But nothing to complain about.'

When he had gone, I could only manage a few mouthfuls before I had to push the plate away. Afterwards, I started reading again, but I was unable to concentrate. All the while my thoughts kept returning to Frank. In one sense, I felt an enormous sense of relief at finally embarking on something that meant so much to him. In another, of course, doing so only made his absence more acute. Not for the first time, it struck me how this excavation was like a form of disinterment.

Yet even as these thoughts ran through my mind, I had a sense of everything fading. Memories fleeing as I attempted to clutch on to them. Still staring at the open book, I recalled how Carter had written that he could remember little or nothing of the actual moment when he had stood looking into the burial chamber. All these impressions had crowded in on him to such an extent that not one of them had lodged. Looking back several months afterwards, he found to his dismay that his mind was quite blank.

Grateley's face was as impassive as always as he cleared my plate away. 'Would you thank Mrs Lyons for me?' I said. 'The beef was delicious. It's just that I don't appear to have much of an appetite at the moment.'

'I expect it is this weather, ma'am.'

'Yes,' I agreed. 'I expect it is.'

'Will there be anything else?'

'No. That will be all, thank you.'

'I'll wish you goodnight, then, ma'am.'

'Goodnight, Grateley.'

Upstairs, I looked in on Robert. Recently, for reasons that are still a mystery to me, he has become obsessed with making drawings of the Matterhorn. When I asked him why, he did not reply. Instead, his shoulders seemed to fold towards one another, as if he was shutting himself from my gaze. These drawings are identical, or nearly identical; I assume because they have been copied out of a book. A number of them had been pinned to the wall. They lifted in the breeze when I opened the door.

Robert was asleep and had thrown off most of the blankets. One of his feet was exposed, the white bulb of his heel sticking up in the air, the toes bent against the mattress.

I covered his foot with one of the blankets, then kissed him on the forehead. He gave a small grunt – it was almost a sigh – but did not stir.

On the following afternoon I was told that Mr Maynard from Ipswich Museum had come to pay a visit – Mr Maynard is the curator of the museum and effectively Mr Reid Moir's deputy. According to Grateley, he had gone straight out to the excavation rather than come to the house and risk disturbing me. I decided that I would also go and see how Mr Brown was getting on.

During the night it had rained and the grass was still slippery. I had to be careful where I put my feet. Hearing a yell, I looked up to see Robert running towards me. Around his head he had what appeared to be an elastic garter with several feathers stuck in it. I watched him come closer, rooted to the spot. All the time I was waiting for him to stop. However, he just kept coming. His arms were outstretched, his mouth open wide and his cheeks full of air.

When he threw his arms around my legs, I reached down and gripped him by the tops of his arms.

'Darling, no,' I said.

I thought that I might fall backwards, that his weight might make me topple over. For a moment it seemed as if his legs were still spinning. As if he had not heard what I had said, or intended to ignore it.

'Darling, no, please,' I said, and pushed him away.

Abruptly, his legs stopped. He looked up at me in confusion, as if everything had just slipped out of true.

'You – you musn't rush everywhere, Robbie. You could easily cause an accident.'

'I'm sorry, Mama,' he said.

Turning round, he walked off towards one of the spoil heaps. Feeling wretched, I watched him go, trying to read his mood from the slope of his shoulders.

Mr Maynard and Mr Brown were standing on the far side of the mound. The first trench now reached all the way to the centre. It was also wider than before; wide enough for two people to stand side by side. At right angles to it was a second trench, narrower than the first, but also reaching to the centre.

Maynard is a bustling, fretful man with a kind of perpetual dampness about him – a result, in part, of his having unusually moist eyes. With the best will in the world, you could never describe him as scintillating company. But at times, when he is being especially literal-minded, there is a small, faraway smile on his face, as if in some private corner of his brain he relishes the effect he is having on others.

After I had greeted the two of them, Mr Brown asked if I might like to see how they were getting along.

I told him I would like that very much.

'But your feet, Mrs Pretty,' said Mr Maynard unhappily. 'I fear they will become muddy.'

'There's no need to worry, Mr Maynard. As you can see, I am wearing quite sturdy shoes.'

It was a strange feeling, stepping into the mound. A rich underground smell rose all around me, of roots, dankness and decay. The mud walls shone with moisture. The

23

imprints of the shovel blades were clearly visible in the earth. So too were the layers of soil, these broad, perpendicular bands on either side. In some places, the walls had already started to crumble. Planks had been placed vertically on the ground to try to prevent them from doing so.

At the far end of the trench was a small pit. At the bottom of it, I could just make out a lighter-coloured patch of soil with ragged, ill-defined edges. The outline had been marked with pegs and baling twine.

Mr Brown pointed at the pit. 'Now, that might be the chamber there. Although I have to tell you it could just as easily be a dew pond, Mrs Pretty. Sometimes it's the devil to tell them apart.'

'Surely the solution is to dig down and find out,' I said.

Mr Brown started to laugh. 'Oh, that's the solution all right. At least that's what I would have said. However, Mr Maynard and I were just having a discussion about the best way to proceed. He is in favour of our digging a third trench here –' He indicated the other side of the mound to the narrower of the two trenches. 'Whereas my instinct under the circumstances is to make do with just the two.'

I turned round to Mr Maynard. He was standing right behind me.

'The normal procedure is to dig three trenches,' he said doggedly. 'That way one can be as sure as possible that nothing is missed. Mr Reid Moir always insists on three – always.'

'I do appreciate that thoroughness is vital, Mr Maynard,' I said. 'And I can assure you that I would never countenance anything slapdash. Yet at the same time one also has to bear in mind that there is a certain amount of urgency about the excavation.'

'Urgency?' He gazed at me with his moist eyes. 'I'm afraid I don't understand.'

'We are at the mercy of factors beyond our control.'

Maynard blinked several times and then lowered his voice. 'You are alluding to the international situation, madam?'

'Exactly.'

A lengthy pause followed, during which Mr Maynard stood quite still. Slowly, as if by infinitesimal degrees, the small, faraway smile came over his face.

I glanced at Mr Brown, who caught my eye. We waited a little longer. At last Mr Maynard said, 'I shall tell Mr Reid Moir that two trenches would appear to be sufficient. Under the present circumstances.'

'Thank you very much, Mr Maynard. That is kind.'

The two of us walked back to the house. Robert came too. He was careful, I noticed, to keep a safe distance away. Every few paces, he jumped in the air and gave a piercing whoop. Then he ran on ahead and waited for Mr Maynard and me to catch him up.

'A delightful boy,' said Maynard. 'Quite charming . . . Do you have many grandchildren, Mrs Pretty?'

'As a matter of fact, Robert is my son,' I told him.

For a pale-skinned man, Maynard changed colour with remarkable speed. His entire face became crimson, even his ears.

'I – I really am most dreadfully sorry.'

'Please do not distress yourself, Mr Maynard,' I said. 'It is a perfectly understandable mistake to make.'

*

25

On Wednesday morning I made my weekly excursion to
London. As usual, Lyons brought the Alvis round to the
front door after breakfast. He was standing outside in his
navy-blue uniform, the sun glinting off his buttons. Robert
came to see me off. I was aware of how heavy my feet
sounded on the gravel, crunching laboriously from step to
step, and of how little noise his own feet made by
comparison.

'Will you be able to amuse yourself while I am away?'
I asked.

'Mr Brown says that I can help with the digging.'

'Does he? Well, just be careful not to –'

'Not to what, Mama?'

I shook my head. 'It doesn't matter.'

After I had kissed him, he remained squinting up at me.

'Is there something wrong, darling?'

'Your hat.'

'What about it?'

He giggled. 'It's on crooked.'

I reached up to straighten it. 'There, is that better?'

'Yes,' he said doubtfully.

On the way into Woodbridge it began to spit with rain.
We became stuck behind a convoy of army trucks. Men in
uniform sat in the back. They gazed out, their white faces
fusing into a single, biddable mass as they swayed from side
to side. The convoy was moving so slowly that I grew
concerned that I should miss my train.

However, when we arrived at the station it turned out
that the train had been cancelled due to a points failure at
Ipswich. As a result, it would be an hour before the next
one. Rather than simply sit and wait, I decided to go for a
walk around the town. I asked Lyons to stay where he was

and told him that I would return shortly. I then set off up Market Street, towards the Bull Hotel.

Halfway up the hill, I stopped briefly in a shop doorway, then looked back down towards the estuary. Despite its being high tide, surprisingly few boats were on the water. Those that were drifted listlessly about, their jibs flapping. I had not gone much further when I became aware of a very disagreeable sensation. I began to suspect that I was being followed. At first, I assumed I must be imagining it and tried to push the thought to the back of my mind. But instead of going away, as I hoped it would, the suspicion steadily hardened.

Once again I stopped and looked back down the street. This time, however, I stayed where I was. Within a matter of seconds, Lyons came round the corner. He saw me immediately, although he tried his best to pretend that he had not. None the less, he had no real choice but to continue walking in my direction. In an attempt to make himself appear more nonchalant, he began to whistle.

When he reached the doorway where I was standing, I stepped out in front of him.

'Mr Lyons . . .'

'Ah!' he said. 'Hello there, ma'am.'

For several moments we stood and regarded one another. I have known Lyons for more than thirty years. He started off working for my father, and when Frank and I moved down to Suffolk, he and his wife came too. In that time, we have developed something of an understanding.

'Mr Lyons, were you by any chance following me?'

Lyons is a naturally gruff man; it does not suit him to look embarrassed. He tilted his face towards the ground until the black peak of his cap was facing me like a great inane smile.

'I do appreciate your concern for my welfare,' I said. 'But I assure you that I can easily manage on my own. Now, will you go and wait by the car, as we arranged? I will not be long – twenty minutes at the most. If I have not returned by then, you have my permission to come and look for me. Does that sound reasonable?'

He agreed that it did sound reasonable and walked off down the hill. Continuing past the Bull and the war memorial, I reached the gate of St Mary's Church. There was a car parked opposite. Although the car was empty, the wiper had been left turned on. It was beating across the windscreen, giving out a dry, squeaking sound. The rubber shuddered against the glass as it went back and forth.

A path lined on both sides by silver limes led to the church door. The door was standing open. Inside, it was much cooler, the rich sweet smell of the blossom replaced by a more ecclesiastical one: old book bindings and wood polish. There was nobody else in the church.

I sat in one of the pews and knelt down, tufts of wiry wool jabbing into my knees. In a niche on one side of the pulpit were three carved figures: the Virgin Mary in the middle, with two faceless saints on either side, their hands clasped over their chests as they both turned stiffly towards her.

I put my hands together, just as I had done as a child, hoping that I might feel once again the same certainties, the same calm surety, that I had felt then. I prayed – for peace, of course, and also for Robert. I know that he is bored. I also suspect that he may be lonely. There are scarcely any children of his own age for him to play with, either on the estate or in the village. My efforts to attract children from Bromeswell and Melton to come to Sutton Hoo House have not been successful. Their parents, I suspect, do not care for the idea.

When I had finished praying for Robert, I prayed for guidance, as well as for some sense, however faint, of a reciprocal fingertip brushing mine. But today, even more than usual, my prayers struggled to stay aloft: clumsy, flightless things, seeking an uncertain destination.

Coming out, I saw that the car was no longer there, although the sound of its shuddering wiper seemed to remain, like a distant echo. Lyons was waiting outside the station, as we had agreed. No doubt he is curious as to what I do on my weekly excursions, although I think it unlikely that he, or indeed anyone else, would be able to guess the real reason for them.

When the train arrived, he helped me on board and found me a seat. Due to the earlier cancellation, it was unusually crowded. Lyons stood on the platform with his arms by his sides, waiting until the train had drawn away.

We must have made an odd-looking procession. First came Lyons, carrying a wicker chair. Then Robert and finally myself. The chair was set up on top of the mound so I could look down into the excavation. Robert sat at my feet, with Lyons squatting on the ground alongside him. It was much colder than it had been the day before, although the clouds were high and almost motionless. I wore my thickest winter overcoat buttoned to my neck, as well as a pair of sheepskin gloves.

By the time we arrived, the men had already started digging. So far, though, they had found nothing apart from a cluster of rabbit skeletons, with the bones all entwined together like a giant bird's nest. Robert hardly moved as he gazed down at the men digging away. Never before have I seen him so rapt, so absorbed in anything. Any concern I had felt about him being a nuisance had been replaced by gratitude that at last he had something to keep him occupied.

The first indication that Mr Brown might have made a discovery was when I saw him crouch down and put his face very close to the ground. Taking his pastry brush out of his back pocket, he began sweeping. His face appeared leaner, more pointed than ever. As he swept away, I found myself feeling a quickening sense of excitement. A spark of hope had been ignited within me and already it was too late to quench it.

I half-pushed myself up on the arms of the wicker chair. 'What is it, Mr Brown?'

'There's something here,' he said, his voice muffled. 'Something, although Chri – heaven only knows what.'

The three of us craned eagerly forward. Mr Brown kept on brushing for several more minutes. Then he sat back. 'Here,' he said.

His index finger was outstretched. 'Can you see? It's a piece of wood. There are blackened patches on it. Something appears to have been burned on top. Probably grave-robbers, lighting a fire to keep warm.'

From where I was sitting, I could just make out the ripple of the grain amid the slick of yellow mud. Robert was leaning so far out that I had to hold on to his hand to make sure he didn't fall into the pit.

'Be careful, darling.'

'But I want to have a look.'

He kept trying to pull away. It was as much as I could do to keep hold of him.

'Just try to be patient. I know that it's not easy.'

For the next hour Mr Brown continued brushing at the earth with his pastry brush. By the time he had finished, the piece of wood had been uncovered and its dimensions measured and written down in an old exercise book that he carried with him.

Mr Brown said that at first he thought it might be a coffin lid. However, he was puzzled by the rounded corners as well as by the upturned edges. It was Spooner, a slaughterman on the Fielding estate at Bardsey before he came to Sutton Hoo House, who said that the upturned edges reminded him of a butcher's tray. Mr Brown decided to try to lift the piece of wood, to see what lay underneath. He asked Spooner, Jacobs and also Lyons to help. Each of them would take a corner.

First, Mr Brown did what he could to prise it free, running a knife blade around the underside. Next, the men practised with two of the planks, holding them side by side, keeping them balanced and properly supported. Once they had done this to Mr Brown's satisfaction, they gathered in the pit.

'Right, lads. On a count of three.'

The first attempt was unsuccessful. So too was the second, as well as the third. The men heaved and groaned, their legs straining, and yet nothing happened. The dampness of the earth seemed to suck at the wood, loath to let it go. But on the fourth attempt, after an even louder exhortation than before from Mr Brown, it finally came free.

'That's it . . . There we go . . . Now, up she comes.'

We watched enthralled as the piece of wood was hoisted slowly into the air. From where I was sitting, it appeared to be perfectly symmetrical. I had my arms around Robert's waist. Now he felt slack against me, like a sack of sand.

The men were still kneeling, just about to stand up, when Mr Brown shouted suddenly, 'Down! Down! Put it down!'

As quickly as they could, the men lowered it back down to the ground. But already it was too late. With no sound at all, the wood separated into two pieces along its length. And then one of them broke across the middle. This time there was a damp, apologetic crack. All three pieces fell to the ground.

Afterwards, the four men stayed on their knees, facing one another. None of them spoke. Mr Brown was the first to move. He climbed out of the pit and headed off in the direction of Top Hat Wood. I could see how angry he was with himself, and how disappointed too. His hands were balled into fists. He held them by his side with his elbows jutting out. Then he began to pace around in a series of tight little circles.

The other three men climbed out of the pit and dusted themselves down. Still nobody had spoken. I thought it best that we should leave. I indicated as much to Lyons and also to Robert, who seemed to understand – certainly he made no protest. Lyons picked up the wicker chair and, in the same order as before, the three of us walked away.

Two letters arrived in the post the next morning. The first was from Mr Reid Moir, asking how the excavation was going. Unfortunately, there was little to report. Further digging beneath the butcher's tray had revealed nothing. Mr Brown had advised that there was no point in continuing. We therefore decided that he should start on another mound. I left the choice of which up to him and resolved to stay away from the excavation until he had something to report.

The second letter was from Miss Price, telling me that she would not now be returning to Sutton Hoo House to continue working as Robert's governess/companion. She apologized profusely for this, but said that she felt she should remain with her family in the West Country.

It was a letter I had been both half-expecting and dreading. Looking up, I met Robert's inquiring gaze. I said nothing, hoping that he had not recognized Miss Price's handwriting. After breakfast, I sat in the sitting room and wondered, inconclusively, what to do.

I have no recollection of falling asleep, or even of feeling particularly tired. The next thing I knew, however, I had awakened to a clamour of voices. Beneath the voices there was another deeper, darker sound, like the growling of bassoons. Through the French window I saw Grateley running across the lawn. I couldn't recall ever having seen him outdoors before. The sunlight seemed to exaggerate his cadaverousness, causing him to skip agitatedly about in his tail coat.

My surprise was compounded by the fact that Ellen was running beside him. The two of them were moving in tandem. As they ran along together, Grateley's hand appeared to slide down her back.

When I rang the bell there was no response. Again I rang the bell, jangling it impatiently from side to side. Finally Mrs Lyons came in. Her hair was white with flour.

'What is happening?' I asked her. 'Has Mr Brown found something? Why was I not informed?'

'Ma'am . . . I believe there has been an accident.'

'An accident? What kind of accident?'

'An accident with the excavation.'

I stood up, fetched my coat from the hallway and hurried outside. As I came close to the mounds, I could see immediately what had happened. A trench had been driven into the second mound, just as it had into the first. However, the whole of one side of this trench had collapsed. A shelf of mud had slid down, covering everything below it. In front of me I could see Jacobs, Spooner, Grateley and Ellen. All of them were kneeling down and digging away at the earth with their hands. Even then, it took me a moment or two to realize that there was no sign of Mr Brown.

'Are you sure you are looking in the right place?' I called out.

'Not sure, no,' said Jacobs, tossing clods over his shoulder. 'Mr Brown was the only one inside when it happened. But we think it was here.'

I knelt down beside them, plunging my hands into the damp earth. Although there were shovels close by, no one dared use them for fear of causing further injuries. Several more minutes went by, with all of us scrabbling away. Still there was no sign of him. Scooping up another handful of earth, I glanced at my wrist watch and tried to calculate how long Mr Brown had been buried for.

And then came a shout from Spooner: 'There's something here!'

I looked up to see that Spooner was holding Mr Brown's cap. We all moved in a circle around the spot where he had found it and continued digging away.

A few minutes later Jacobs found Mr Brown's hand. It was sticking out of the earth, his fingers bent and splayed, his cuff still buttoned at the wrist. The men took hold of his wrist and pulled. As they did so, Mr Brown slid out of the ground towards them. There was mud in his eye sockets and in his nostrils. His skin had a yellowish tinge.

Spooner pinched the mud away. Meanwhile, Jacobs put an ear to his chest. Mr Brown was not breathing. His chest was quite still. Jacobs sat astride him and began pumping away. Still nothing happened. Jacobs leaned forward, putting his mouth over Mr Brown's and trying to force air into his lungs. He waited a few seconds and tried again.

In desperation, he began to pound Mr Brown with his fists, hitting him so hard I feared he might break his ribs.

'Come on, Basil!' he shouted. 'Come back!'

Still there was no response. Beside me, Ellen started to cry. Jacobs rocked back on to his heels. Just as he did so, a shiver passed all the way along Mr Brown's body. He started to shake; his back was bucking, his legs jerking up and down. He gave a long, hacking cough and sucked noisily for air.

I felt such a sense of relief that it made my head spin. Meanwhile, Grateley had fetched some water. He held a tin cup to Mr Brown's lips, tipping it up. The cup rattled against his teeth. Most of the water ran out of the side of his mouth. Some, though, he managed to swallow.

For several more minutes he lay there, his breathing becoming less tremulous. Then he raised himself up on one elbow. He looked at each of us, blinking the mud away.

'Damn . . .' he said. 'Damn and blast.' His voice was faint, but perfectly clear.

'Just lie back and try to relax,' I told him.

He took no notice of this. Holding on to Jacobs's sleeve,

he tried to force it downwards towards him. At the same time, his feet started paddling round, churning up the dirt.

'What on earth are you doing, Mr Brown?'

His feet continued to spin feebly as he clutched at Grateley. 'Be fine once I'm standing,' he said.

'You will do no such thing. Do you understand me?'

'Yes, you just listen to Mrs Pretty, Basil,' said Spooner.

But again he took no notice. With some difficulty, Jacobs managed to unclench Mr Brown's fingers from his sleeve. Looking greatly offended, Mr Brown fell back on to the ground.

'Could you find something to carry him to the house on?' I said to the men.

In the end they used a tarpaulin, rolling Mr Brown over on to the centre of it. He was so light that the three of them had no difficulty in carrying him; the tarpaulin scarcely sagged in the middle as they did so. I asked them to take him into the sitting room and lay him on the sofa. Then I went to the cloakroom to wash my hands and to fill a jug of water.

When I came back, once again Mr Brown tried to stand up, swinging his legs over the side of the sofa. Immediately, they crumpled beneath him and he collapsed on to the cushions.

'Mr Brown, kindly do as you are told. You are clearly suffering from shock. And quite possibly from concussion.'

He did not reply to this, but lay there, looking up at the ceiling with his lips pressed together. A few moments later his chest began heaving again. Immediately afterwards, he started to retch. A stream of coffee-coloured vomit spurted on to the carpet.

As he was being sick, I sat beside him, holding the back of his head. Once he had finished, I gave him some more water to drink before fetching a bowl and a cloth and wiping up the vomit.

'So sorry,' he said.

'There is no need to apologize.'

Once again he started to shake, emitting a series of faint moans as he did so. Breaths bubbled and burst on his lips. When the shaking subsided, he lay back and stared at the ceiling through unblinking eyes. I gave him more water to drink. I could hear the gurgle as it passed down his throat. We both waited to see if it would come back up. When he was confident that it would not, Mr Brown started to say something else.

'Try not to speak,' I told him.

However, his lips continued working away. 'Rabbits,' he said eventually – the word seeming to topple out of the side of his mouth.

'Rabbits, Mr Brown?'

'Rabbits,' he repeated, more firmly this time. 'I told you they were bad for excavation, didn't I?'

'You did indeed, although I don't believe this is the time to go through all that again.'

'It was my fault,' he continued. 'I should have cut back terraces. I was trying to save time, you see. That way everything has less far to fall. The earth, it moves so quickly, though. I reckoned I was a goner there.'

Briefly his eyes clouded over. He shut them tight. A few moments later he opened them again. When they had regained focus, he looked carefully round the room and then at me, as if for the first time.

'You shouldn't be doing this, Mrs Pretty,' he said.

'Doing what?'

'This!'

'Believe me, Mr Brown, I have dealt with far worse cases than yours.'

'What do you mean?'

'I was an auxiliary nurse during the war.'

'You were? How's that, then?'

'I worked in a local hospital near my family home in Lancashire. Soldiers from France were sent back there. At least the ones who were fit to travel. Now, is there anyone you want me to notify, to tell them you are all right? Forgive me, I don't even know if you are married.'

'I am married,' he said. 'To May.'

'Would you like me to pass on a message to her? I could easily send a telegram.'

'No need.'

'Are you sure? I wouldn't want her hearing anything from anyone else and worrying unduly.'

He shook his head. 'She's not the worrying type.'

There was a blanket folded on one of the chairs that I occasionally used to cover my legs. I covered Mr Brown with it. 'Now I'd like you to remain here for as long as you want. If you wish to sleep, by all means do so. When you are ready to move, or if you would care for something to eat, just ring the bell. I'll leave it by you, here.'

After placing the bell on the table beside him, I walked across to the door. But before I had a chance to open it, he started to say something else. Thinking he was about to start apologizing again, I asked, or rather told, him to stop.

'No, no.' He waved his hand dismissively. 'Not that.'

'What is it?'

He paused, then said, 'I hoped I might see something.'

'See something?'

'When I was buried.'

'I don't understand.'

'I thought I might see something . . . A sign or something. Like the Angel of Mons . . . You know, something like that.'

'And did you?'

Again he shook his head. 'There was nothing. Only darkness.'

When I went to say goodnight to Robert he was sitting up in bed. He had done some more drawings of the Matterhorn, I saw. Now they spilled over on to a second wall of his bedroom.

'Is Mr Brown going to die, Mama?' he asked.

'No, Robbie.'

'Are you sure?'

'Absolutely positive.'

'Oh,' he said, sounding disappointed.

'I thought you liked Mr Brown.'

'I do like him.'

'Would you like me to read you a story?'

He brightened immediately. 'Yes, please.'

I picked up a copy of *Tales of the Greek Heroes* from the pile of books beside his bed and opened it at the story of Orpheus and Eurydice. I read how Orpheus loved his wife, Eurydice, so much that after she died from a snakebite he went down into the underworld to try to bring her back into the realm of the living.

' "At the River Styx the dark old ferryman, Charon, was waiting with his boat. He was only allowed to ferry dead souls across that stream and they paid him one coin, called an 'obol', which was always placed ready in a dead person's mouth. Normally, Charon would have refused to take this living passenger, but Orpheus played so sweetly for him on

his harp that he relented. On the other side, Orpheus found
himself in the grey, twilit land of the dead, where ghosts
flitted about, moaning and gibbering.'' '

'Mama . . .' said Robert.

'Yes, darling.'

'Does Mr Brown always wear the same clothes?'

'I have no idea.'

'Do you think he ever changes his underthings?'

'I'm quite sure he does.'

'But you can't be sure.'

'Would you like me to read some more, Robbie, or are
you going to go to sleep now?'

'I don't mind.'

After I had closed the book, I lit the candle by his bed
and turned off the light. Robert, however, remained sitting
up in bed, with the candle burning beside him. Something
about the way the shadows fell on his cheekbones made me
imagine, just for a moment, that it was Frank gazing back
at me. Gravely and with a hint of reproof. Then the
shadows shifted and he instantly reverted to being a child.

'Mama . . .'

'Yes, darling.'

'Do you think Mr Brown will find any treasure?'

'I really don't know.'

'But you still hope he might?'

'I still hope so, yes.'

'I hope so too,' he said.

'Although we mustn't depend upon it, you know.'

'I know that.'

'Goodnight, Robbie. I'll see you in the morning.'

'Goodnight, Mama.'

*

I lay in bed and listened to the wireless. There was a talk on clothes through the centuries. This was followed by a dance by Wendy Toye entitled *The Blue Madonna* and set to the music of 'Air on a G String'. When it was over, I turned out the light and lay there, hoping sleep would come. It did not; my mind would not let it.

After I had been lying for two or three hours, the house began to creak. The man we bought the house from, a Mr Lomax, imported timber from the Far East, hence all the wood panelling. Whenever the temperature drops, the wood contracts. It sounds as if the entire house is twisting on its foundations. I lay there for a little longer, then put on my dressing gown and slippers and went across to the window.

When I drew back the curtain, the garden was white with moonlight. I could see all the way down to the river. The moon itself was reflected in the surface of the water. Even in the reflection, I was able to make out the dark smudges of the lunar seas.

I sat on the window seat, staring out. Trying to ward off thoughts that came towards me like flocks of angry birds. One memory in particular kept returning: Robert running across the grass with his arms stretched out and his cheeks full of air. And then my pushing him away. I know that I am failing him. The awareness sits there, like a weight on my shoulders, pressing down. Constantly reminding me that whatever capacity I once possessed for motherhood is disappearing.

All that seems left is this ever-widening gap between the scale of my devotion and my ability to succour him. To protect him. It feels as if I am standing on the brink of his world, forever on the threshold and yet unable to step across. Yearning to match his vigour, his boisterousness, but lacking either the imagination or the resources to do so on my own.

After a while I went to check on him. It was quite bright in the corridor; light was shining in through the oriel window. I stood outside Robert's room, listening. I could hear his breathing. Slow and apparently untroubled.

With no purpose in mind, beyond a vague desire not to remain stationary, I started to walk down the corridor – away from my room. Everything was quiet now; the house had stopped creaking. The strip of carpet stretched out before me. Although I was wide awake, I had a strange feeling that I was sleepwalking. My slippered feet seemed to develop a rhythm of their own. I went through one doorway, then another.

Soon I was in a part of the house that was scarcely ever used. Even when Frank was alive, we seldom came here, except on the rare occasions when we had guests. On either side, doors led off into bedrooms that no one had ever slept in – at least not in our time.

When I reached the far end of the corridor, I turned round, intending to retrace my steps. It was at that point that I heard something. A knocking sound. Quite regular, like someone marking out time with a baton. It was coming from the room to my left.

To my surprise, the door was ajar. Coming the other way, I had not noticed it. But now I could see a narrow gap between the door and the frame. A right-angled band of silvery light. Meanwhile, the sound continued: regular, metronomic beats, tapping away.

I pushed the door open. The room was as white as the garden outside. It might have been filled with hoar frost.

The noise was louder now, much louder than I had expected. So loud that I saw the cause of it immediately. For some reason, the window was open and the wooden end of the curtain cord was swinging about, banging against the wall.

Crossing the room, I closed the window. It slid shut quite easily. Only then did I notice that the bed had been made. All the other beds in all the other rooms had been left stripped – there was no reason to do otherwise. This one, though, had unmistakably been made. I could see the sheets pulled up over the pillows, as well as a square of blanket neatly folded at the foot of the bed.

I also thought that I could smell a very faint aroma; it seemed to be threaded through the air. Perfume, but with something else too. Something more medicinal, like liniment.

When I turned on the light, the brightness made my eyes shrink. But even in that first flash of illumination, I saw something else. The bed was not only made; there were two imprints there. Two figures had lain there. The outlines of their forms were clearly visible in the pillows, as well as on the contours of the sheets. Also in two small, rounded depressions on the centre of the folded blanket.

Sitting down on the foot of the bed, I put my hand on the linen sheet. It was cold to the touch. On the table beside the bed were a mug and a teacup. The mug was not one I had seen before. It was made of brown earthenware with a narrow glazed silver band around the rim. There was what appeared to be the outline of a lip on the silver rim.

On the side of the mug was a picture of a man sitting astride a horse. Beneath it was a printed rhyme:

> Tom Pearce, Tom Pearce, lend me your grey mare
> All along, down along, out along lee
> For I want to go to Widdecombe Fair
> Wi' Bill Brewer, Jan Stewer, Peter Gurney,
> Peter Davy, Dan'l Widdon, 'Arry 'Awk,
> Old Uncle Tom Cobbley and all,
> Old Uncle Tom Cobbley and all.

In the morning I awoke in my own bed with no memory of how I had got back there. When I sat up, I saw there was even more of my hair lying on the pillow than usual. I flushed it away before Ellen came.

It is pointless pretending that my spirits lifted at the news that Mr Reid Moir and Mr Maynard had come to visit. I felt so tired I had been hoping to have the morning alone. However, I could hardly refuse to see them.

Mr Reid Moir was a tailor before he became a palaeontologist. As a result, he is always immaculately turned out. Today, he was wearing a dove-grey suit with a matching tie. In his hand he held a book. Although he is a tall, well-built man, he is very light and fluent on his feet. There is a suppleness about his body generally that goes with his air of lacquered sensuality. Mr Maynard followed him through the door, a couple of steps behind.

'Mrs Pretty,' Reid Moir murmured. 'Always a pleasure.'

I asked them to sit down. They did so, on opposite ends of the sofa. Glancing down at the carpet, I was relieved to see there was no evidence of Mr Brown's having been sick.

'How may I be of assistance, gentlemen?'

'It's about Brown,' said Reid Moir.

'Yes? What about Mr Brown?'

I thought at first they had come to inquire about his health. This, however, turned out not to be the case. 'There is a project the museum is involved with over at Stanton,' Reid Moir went on. 'A Roman villa. It's a project we are hoping to complete before – should hostilities commence. Brown was working at Stanton before he came here. In fact, he did so on the understanding that he would return there once he had finished. Without wishing to beat about the bush, we rather hoped he would be back by now.'

'I had no idea Mr Brown was here on loan,' I said.

'Not on loan, Mrs Pretty.' Reid Moir smiled agreeably, while crossing one leg over the other. 'I would hardly put it like that. But I understand that, despite everyone's best efforts, progress here has been limited. And we felt that this might be a good moment to recall him, as it were.'

'Surely that is up to Mr Brown? You would need to speak to him.'

'We have spoken to him,' interjected Maynard.

Reid Moir turned to Maynard. He remained staring at him until Maynard changed colour, then he turned back to me.

'We did happen to have a quick word with him before we came here,' he acknowledged.

'And what did he say?'

'Brown is a very uncomplicated man,' said Reid Moir. 'He sees the world in starkly black and white terms. That, of course, is one of his great virtues. His attitude is that, as you are paying his wages, his allegiance is to you.'

'But you do not see it that way, Mr Reid Moir?'

'I too am an uncomplicated man, Mrs Pretty – in my way. My only interest is the welfare of the museum. As I say, the excavation at Stanton is an important one. If successful, and we have, I believe, ample grounds for optimism, it might considerably increase our understanding of the entire Roman occupation of Suffolk. In the light of current events, one has to balance that against a more, you will forgive me for being frank, minor venture. One that, while fascinating in many respects, has so far failed to yield anything of significance.'

Possibly lack of sleep had made me irritable, possibly not. 'Let me make sure I understand you clearly, Mr Reid Moir,' I said. 'You are suggesting that Mr Brown should leave my employ forthwith and resume working for you at Stanton.'

'Not for me, Mrs Pretty,' said Reid Moir with an indulgent laugh. 'For the museum. Always the museum . . .'

'Do forgive me.'

He gave an absolving tip of the head.

'I am aware that the excavation here must strike you as a very silly, even an indulgent affair,' I said.

Reid Moir started to speak, but evidently thought better of it.

'I do hope, though, that you will be able to humour me a little,' I went on. 'After all, I have been an enthusiastic and, I trust, helpful patron of the museum in the past.'

'Indeed you have, Mrs Pretty. Indeed . . .'

'Perhaps, therefore, I might presume on your goodwill for a little longer.'

He remained quite still, with one stationary foot arched upwards.

'How much longer did you have in mind, Mrs Pretty?' he asked.

Looking through the window, I saw that it had begun to rain. The rain clattered on the ivy leaves outside and kicked up little spouts of mud in the flower beds.

'I would like Mr Brown to excavate one more mound for

me. Then, when he has finished doing so, he will be free to go back to Stanton.'

'One more mound?' said Reid Moir, his voice a little less lacquered than before. 'You mean, another one entirely?'

'That is correct.'

'But that could take – goodness – another three weeks. Perhaps even longer if this weather doesn't clear. While I naturally do not want you to feel under pressure, Mrs Pretty, I must point out that any protracted delay might jeopardize a potentially important find. The site at Stanton could well prove to be the largest Roman villa north of Felixstowe.'

We gazed at one another. 'Perhaps I have not made myself clear,' I said. 'I would like Mr Brown to excavate one more mound.'

Reid Moir stared back at me. His gaze was direct, his foot still carefully crooked. Even with the door closed, I could hear the grandfather clock ticking in the hallway.

'However, I do not wish to be unreasonable,' I went on. 'If Mr Brown has not found anything by the end of next week, say, then I shall release him to do your bidding.'

This time he barely hesitated. 'By the end of next week . . . The end of the month, as it happens. Very well, then.'

'I am grateful for your indulgence, Mr Reid Moir,' I said. 'Now, was there anything else you wished to talk about?'

'As a matter of fact there was.' He held out the book he had with him. 'I thought you might care for a copy of my latest work.'

'How very kind.'

'It's about flints.'

'Flints?' I repeated, sounding rather more surprised than I might have wished.

47

'With particular reference to the Cromer field bed in Norfolk.'

'I shall greatly look forward to reading it,' I told him.

He uncrossed his legs and stood up. Maynard followed suit. At the front door I wished them goodbye. Reid Moir lowered his eyelashes, while Maynard gave a mournful-looking smile.

It continued to rain throughout the day. Robert stayed indoors and played with his train set in the nursery. He insisted that he was perfectly happy on his own, even claiming that he preferred it. From downstairs, I could hear the noise of the engine going round and round the track. I found I could not wait for the day to end. Both of us went to bed even earlier than usual.

The following morning the weather had barely improved. Despite the rain, Mr Brown had insisted on returning to work. Together with Jacobs and Spooner, he removed the earth that had buried him, placed planks along the side of the trench to ensure that there were no further landslides and continued with his excavation.

At eight thirty Mr Lyons drove me into Woodbridge to catch the London train. On the journey I started to read Mr Reid Moir's book about flints. However, I am afraid I found it rather heavy going and put it aside after only a few pages.

When we reached Liverpool Street, I queued for a taxi and asked to be taken to Earls Court. As we drove down the Strand, I was aware of a strange atmosphere of gaiety, of excitement. A tightening in the air that I had not noticed before. People sauntered along the pavements and peered into shop windows as they had always done, the men in shirtsleeves and the women in blouses. Yet there seemed to be something exaggerated, something not wholly plausible, about their nonchalance. They moved like loosely knotted figures who at any moment might snap into rigidity.

The cabbie told me that on the previous evening there had been an air-raid drill near to his home in Battersea. A warden had driven round the streets, throwing out different-coloured tennis balls from his car. Yellow and green balls denoted gas; red denoted high explosives, while those with red stripes represented incendiary bombs. The exercise, said the cabbie, laughing delightedly, had been a fiasco. Despite the warden's entreaties, people had immediately picked up the balls and begun throwing them at one another.

In Hyde Park, trenches had been dug. A mass of zigzagging lines now fanned out from Speaker's Corner. In order to dig the trenches, a great many trees had also been felled. Several of the stumps were still sticking out of the ground. The wood looked very soft and white, like chicken flesh.

Further down the Bayswater Road, on the western side of the Serpentine, I was astonished to see that an enormous crater had appeared. This crater must have been forty feet deep and easily twice that across. Around the top the earth was dark brown, shading down to yellow at the bottom. On the road beside it was a queue of cars. Several of them were towing trailers.

Without my asking, the cabbie leaned back and told me that twenty sites had been identified around London where large deposits of sand could be found. People were being encouraged to fill sandbags and place them around the doors and windows of their properties. As yet, however, scarcely anyone had bothered to do so.

He dropped me in Nevern Square. Certainly there were no sandbags here, or any other signs of preparation. Everything appeared just the same as always: the same orange-brick terraces with their long, sceptical-looking windows, the same flowerpots with stiff and crinkled blossoms, the same clusters of unpolished bells beside the front doors.

I rang the bell of Mr Swithin's flat. He was waiting by his front door when I came out of the lift and led the way down the corridor into his living room. As usual he sat at the end of a gate-legged table while I sat on his left. The wallpaper was patterned with an endlessly repeated trellis of bamboo, relieved only by a circular mirror above the fireplace and four chalk drawings of Sealyham terriers on the wall facing me.

For a few minutes Mr Swithin chattered away about the news and the weather. He did so almost apologetically, as if he knew quite well that I had no real interest in talking to him directly.

Eventually, he entwined his fingers, leaned forward on his elbows and peered into that shadow world through which threads of personality run like just-dissolving colours. I knew not to take too much notice of those spirits who came through first of all. As in life, it was the ones who were keenest to make themselves heard who invariably had the least to say. But only when they had spoken their fill could others, less frivolous and more diffident, be allowed to take their place.

Whenever I try to imagine the afterlife, I find myself envisaging an anxious, shiftless crowd. Lines of colourless people queuing endlessly for a series of public telephone boxes where operators, struggling with defective equipment and only able to speak a few phrases of their language, attempt to connect them to whoever awaits their call.

It is not a happy picture, however much I try to bathe it in an appropriately amber glow. Yet somewhere in there, too courteous to make a fuss or to shoulder his way to the front, is Frank. Of that I have no doubt. In time, he must come through. It is just a matter of being patient, of not expecting too much. In the meantime, though, there are only stray phrases and occasional glimpses to sustain me. A thimbleful of endearment. A familiar white line of parting on a head unaccountably twisted aside. Nothing more. Or rather nothing except for the same amorphous blanket of reassurance, the same anonymous balm.

But today nothing seemed to be strained through the trelliswork. Nothing that anyone with a modicum of discrimination could permit themselves to latch on to.

Mr Swithin offered a young man with beautiful hands and a port-wine stain down one side of his face. 'He's mumbling a little,' he said, 'although I can see his face quite clearly.'

'I have no recollection of anyone like that.'

Swiftly, he transferred his attention elsewhere.

'An older lady with an ample bosom who always took particular care with her appearance?' Mr Swithin spoke with the regretful air of a butcher who knows that all his choicest cuts have already been taken.

I shook my head.

'Are you quite sure?' he asked. 'It can often take some time to work out a connection.'

'Quite sure.'

We continued to sit there. Mr Swithin's fingers flexed hopefully away, while the Sealyhams gazed down from the wall. We carried on like this for another twenty minutes. In the end, Mr Swithin said, 'I don't appear to be having much luck today, I'm afraid. Sometimes it's just like being lost in a fog.'

Pushing his chair back, he escorted me down the corridor. I glanced into the kitchen as we went past. On the table, two pork chops lay sandwiched between glass plates. At the door Mr Swithin stopped and exhaled. I took two half-crowns from my purse. Pocketing them in one fluid movement, he asked if he should expect me at the same time next week.

I told him that this might not be convenient – just at that moment I was not sure if I could face any more disappointment. But I could see my terseness had upset Mr Swithin; it's not for nothing that he calls himself a sensitive. Softening my tone, I said, 'Perhaps I could telephone you when I have decided.'

'Of course.'

He stood aside, holding the door by its top corner so that I had to pass underneath the arch of his arm. In the lift, I sat down on the bench seat as it made its descent. When it reached the ground floor, I found I scarcely had the strength to pull back the gates. Slowly, I descended the steps to the pavement.

Once there, I held on to a railing for support. As soon as I had done so, I found that I did not dare take my hand away. Everything tipped and lurched around me. People walked past. One or two of them glanced in my direction without appearing to notice anything unusual. Several minutes went by and still this tipping sensation continued. I began to wonder what I was going to do.

I could not help thinking that I was being punished somehow, principally for my lack of faith. This was what happened to people who did not believe, or who did not believe enough. They were cast out, abandoned, left struggling to fend for themselves.

Despite the sunshine, the railing was very cold to the touch. So cold that I seemed to be losing all feeling in my fingers. Reaching behind me, I transferred my grip from one hand to the other. At that moment, a taxi cab turned off the Earls Court Road and drove into the square. The leap of hope that this brought with it was immediately dashed when I saw that its 'For Hire' sign was not illuminated.

Then, as the taxi continued to come closer, I noticed that nobody was sitting in the back.

I held up my spare hand and waited. The taxi drove round the remaining two sides of the square and drew up beside the kerb. I remained where I was, unsure how I was ever going to cross the expanse of pavement that lay between us. It was like having to ford a stream.

The cabbie sat waiting behind the steering wheel, staring straight ahead, his motor idling. Still, I could not bring myself to let go. The cabbie turned to look at me, his brow knotting into a question mark. As he did so, I launched myself, quite certain that I would fall – yet finding my legs scurrying about beneath me, carrying me forward.

Once inside the taxi, I asked to be taken to Liverpool Street. The journey seemed to pass in a long horizontal blur. By the time we had arrived, however, everything seemed to have righted itself: the buildings, the lamp-posts, even the people. Even so, I found that I had no desire to be in any closer proximity to anyone than necessary. I therefore bought a first-class ticket and shut myself away in an empty compartment, hoping that nobody else would come in. Mercifully, no one did.

The train steamed through deep brick gulches and out towards the suburbs. When the houses at last disappeared, an enormous sense of relief came over me as all around the fields flattened and stretched away.

Ellen was unusually quiet that evening. She scarcely spoke as she helped me out of my travelling clothes and into my dinner dress. I was touched by her tact, by the way she moved around me in this understanding silence.

It was only while she was fastening the buttons on my sleeves that I noticed her fingers were trembling.

'What is it, my dear?'

She did not answer; she simply continued fastening my buttons.

'There we are,' she said, pulling my cuffs straight once she had finished. While her voice sounded steady enough, there was some uncertainty about her lower lip.

'Has something upset you?' I asked. Still she did not answer. 'If there is anything you wish to tell me, I can promise that nothing will go any further than this room.'

At this, she pulled back abruptly. 'There's nothing the matter with me, ma'am,' she said. 'Nothing at all . . . Although it's very kind of you to ask.'

I stood and waited by the mirror while Ellen fetched the clothes brush. She wielded the brush with her customary dexterity, only just letting the bristles touch the material. While she was doing so, I realized it had been several days since she had asked if I would like my hair combed before dinner. Perhaps this too was a form of tact.

The following afternoon it started to rain again. When I went out to the mounds after tea, I found Mr Brown by himself in the shepherd's hut. Immediately, he offered to come outside, but I told him that I was quite happy to join him. He helped me up the steps, shook out my umbrella and swept a place clean with his hand for me to sit.

Jacobs and Spooner, it turned out, had already left for the day, it being impossible to do any further digging in this weather.

I had barely sat down when Mr Brown said, 'I don't think there's anything there, Mrs Pretty.' He spoke in more of a rush than usual, as if this was something he'd been brooding on for some time and wished to get off his chest.

'Are you sure?'

'Not sure, no. But I've got a feeling, if you like.'

'Is that what your nose is telling you?'

'I'm afraid so.'

The sense of dejection was even stronger than I had expected. It seemed to sweep through me like a river, pushing everything aside.

'What do you suggest, then, Mr Brown?' I asked.

'I don't rightly know. That's what I've been thinking about. Trying to work out what's best.'

He appeared just as downcast as I was. We sat in silence for a while. Partly in order to give myself something else to think about and partly because it was something that had made me curious for some time, I asked how he had first become interested in archaeology.

'My granddad used to do a bit of scratching about,' he said. 'Just as a hobby, mind. Then my dad taught me about soil. He'd made a special study of it – Suffolk soil. He knew just about everything there was to know. They said you could show him a handful from anywhere in the county and he could tell you whose farm it had come from.'

'How extraordinary.'

'When I was fifteen, I received a certificate signed by Arthur Mee himself, saying that I had a reliable knowledge of geography, geology and astronomy. After I left school, I tried all sorts of things – farming, keeping goats, being a milkman. I even sold insurance for a while. Trouble was, I couldn't stick at anything. I spent all my time reading, anything I could find. It scarcely mattered what. May says I have far too many books. They nearly drive her mental.'

'And how did you meet Mr Maynard?'

'I met Mr Maynard at the Suffolk Institute. The Reverend Harris from Thornden introduced us. Do you know the Reverend Harris?'

I shook my head.

Mr Brown chuckled. 'He reads even more than me, the reverend does. About archaeology especially. And scripture, of course. I'd done some digging of my own by then. Mainly around the Roman kilns at Wattisfield. Mr Maynard asked if I might like to do some freelance work for the museum. Bits and pieces, you know. Whatever they chose to send my way.'

We sat and listened to the rain falling on the roof. The smell of wet grass came up through the floorboards. Mr Brown was sitting with his elbows resting on his knees.

'I wonder if I might ask a question, Mrs Pretty,' he said.

'By all means.'

'It's just – it's just that I can't help thinking, why now?'

'I'm afraid I don't follow you.'

'Well, I'm wondering to myself why you want the mounds excavating now. After all, it's not as if you've just arrived here, or anything like that.'

As soon as he had finished speaking he glanced away. I suspected he thought he might have overstepped the mark.

'You are quite right, of course,' I said. 'I often discussed it with my late husband. It was a subject that greatly interested us both. But unfortunately he died before we were able to make a start. Then, after he died, I found that it did not seem appropriate somehow. As for what changed my mind, I can only say that I felt that if I did not do it now, then it might be too late.'

He nodded several times. Slowly, the sound of the rain died away. When it had stopped completely, he said, 'Shall we go outside and take a look?'

The air was warm and humid. Steam was already rising from the mounds and the surrounding fields. In places, the rain had beaten the barley flat, the stalks snapped through. The expanses of exposed earth were dotted about with brown puddles.

We stepped around the puddles, scattering rabbits as we went, and walked over to the largest of the mounds. It rose before us, a good four or five feet taller than the others, with a bulkier, much less graceful shape.

'I know you've always fancied this one, Mrs Pretty.'

'Yes, but plainly there is no point in excavating it if you are sure it has already been robbed.'

'Even so, let's have another look, shall we?'

As he had done on our first meeting together, Mr Brown ran up the side of the mound, his feet sliding on the wet grass. When he had reached the summit, he stood there, looking down, with his hands on his hips. Then, as before, he vanished. Just when I was beginning to wonder what had happened to him, he reappeared.

'No, it's definitely a flute, Mrs Pretty. Deeper than most

too, so it looks as if they must have dug quite a wide shaft.'

He started to come back down. But after only a couple of steps, he stopped. I thought at first that he must have caught his foot in a rabbit hole. Then, turning around, he climbed back up. Once at the top of the mound, he began to pace, very deliberately, around its circumference.

When he did come down, he scarcely looked where he put his feet, slithering the last part of the way. Then he started pacing, just as deliberately, around the base of the mound. First, he went one way and then the other. As he was on his second circuit, I saw that his face had taken on the same pointed look he had had when he found the butcher's tray. I heard something too: his tongue had begun clicking against the roof of his mouth,

'What is it, Mr Brown?' I asked.

Instead of answering, he ran back up the mound, remaining there for several minutes with his hand cupping his chin. This time, when he came down again, he did so more slowly. At the bottom he began filling his pipe.

'I suppose you are eventually going to tell me what is on your mind,' I said.

'It may be nothing, Mrs Pretty. Nothing at all. But I happened to notice that this mound is not symmetrical. If you look down from the top, it's more obvious than it is here. You'd expect it to be circular, like the others. But it's not. It's more oval, like a hog's back.'

'Is that relevant?'

'All the other mounds are symmetrical. Why not this one?'

'Perhaps whoever constructed it simply made a mistake.'

'Mmm . . . But that doesn't make sense, does it? Not if you think about it. This is the biggest mound of all. It's the only one you can see from the river. Even on a day like today, it's clearly visible from the opposite bank. Surely they would take more trouble over it. Not less.'

'What is your explanation?'

'Not an explanation, Mrs Pretty. Just a theory, that's all. What if the mound was originally symmetrical? At some stage, this land must have been ploughed up. After all, everywhere else round here has been. That ditch over there –' he pointed towards the road – 'that looks like a medieval field boundary to me. And there's also another one running along the edge of the wood. What if whoever ploughed the land knocked a bit off the mound, as it were. Nobody would have noticed, still less cared. By the time the robbers came along, they would have sunk a shaft into what they thought was the centre of the mound. Or so it would have appeared to them. But it might not have been the centre at all.'

'Let me make quite sure I understand you, Mr Brown. You are saying that while the mound has been robbed, or an attempt has been made to rob it, the thieves might have been looking in the wrong place.'

'That's about the gist of it, yes. Course, I might be wrong.'

'But you might conceivably be right.'

'It's a possibility,' he allowed.

'I see . . . But I have told Mr Reid Moir that you will be free to go to Stanton by the end of the week.'

'We should have an idea by Saturday,' he said. 'One way or another.'

'What do you think, then, Mr Brown? Would you care to attack it?'

He cupped a match over the bowl of his pipe. The

tobacco lit with a hiss and he blew out a mouthful of smoke.

'No harm in trying, is there?'

That evening I ate all the food on my plate, as well as a piece of Cheddar cheese afterwards. As Grateley was taking the plate away and after I had asked him to thank Mrs Lyons, I said, 'It has come to my notice that a member of staff has been using one of the bedrooms upstairs.'

He did not falter. 'A member of staff, ma'am?'

'Or rather two members of staff.'

'Two members of staff?'

'There is no need to repeat everything I say, Grateley. I do not know who is responsible, nor do I intend to make any effort to find out. However, I do not wish this to happen again. Will you make my feelings on the matter known?'

'Of course. Certainly I will, ma'am.'

With my plate in his hand, he moved across to the sideboard. Before he reached it, I said, 'By the way, Grateley, I have not inquired for some time, how is your lumbago?'

He stopped in mid-pace.

'My lumbago? It is very much better, thank you, ma'am.'

'Good. I am pleased to hear that. And do be sure to give my regards to Mrs Grateley,' I added.

His composure was badly holed by now. 'I – I will indeed, ma'am,' he said.

No more hurriedly than usual, although rather less fluently, Grateley gathered up the serving dishes. He disappeared through the swing door with one long leg trailing behind him.

*

My efforts to find Robert a new governess have proved
fruitless. Several of those who had advertised in the
newspaper did not even reply when I wrote back to them.
None of those that did sounded remotely suitable. There
are noticeably fewer advertisements than usual for domestic
positions; no doubt people are loath to think of new jobs at
such a time.

Mr Brown, I am afraid, has found nothing. Nothing
except for a few minute fragments of blue glass and some
splinters of bone. These have been packaged up and sent off
to the museum in Ipswich for analysis. The work is taking
longer than anticipated – due in part to the size of the
mound. It has been, he says, like digging into the side of a
small mountain.

By the end of the third day it was plain that all three men
were not just tired but disillusioned. I noticed they seldom
talked to one another any more when they were working.
At their break times they sat around looking contemplative
and glum. Mr Brown, in particular, is taking it all
personally, plainly feeling that his failure to find anything is
a reflection on his competence. As for Jacobs and Spooner,
I suspect they cannot wait for Saturday to come around and
for the excavation to be over.

Still it has continued to rain, this incessant, lowering,
half-hearted drizzle. But instead of clearing the air, the rain
merely seems to make it even heavier. My fingers have
swollen, the joints in particular. If I was to take off my
rings, I doubt I would be able to put them on again.

Robert too has been affected, by both the weather and
the general atmosphere. He seems listless, devoid of
enthusiasm. At luncheon today he scarcely said a word,
while his appetite, I noticed, was almost as poor as mine.

Afterwards he said he was going outside to see Mr Brown and the men. However, the tone of his voice suggested this would be as much of a chore as everything else.

In the afternoon, I went to Frank's study and sat at his desk. Even if it were not for its associations, I think this would be my favourite room in the house; it seems to hold the daylight longer than any of the others. I had been intending to sort through his papers; there are still some bundles that have not been properly collated.

But once there I found I had neither the resolve nor the energy even to make a start. Clouds sat above the estuary, so grey and low it was virtually impossible to tell where the water ended and the sky began. Only a thin pencil line separated them.

On the shelf above Frank's desk was a pigskin-framed photograph of the two of us on horseback. We were both wearing our riding clothes, both gazing impassively at the camera.

I took the photograph down. It had been taken twelve years ago on a pony-trekking holiday in Iceland. Together, we had ridden across a great plateau in the north of the country, a region referred to in our Baedeker as 'The Uninhabited Highlands'. These highlands were renowned for a type of lichen that was reputed to glow in the dark. Both Frank and I had been rather sceptical about this. Our Icelandic guide, however, insisted that it was well worth seeing, even though it meant we would have to spend the night under canvas.

Setting out in the early afternoon, the three of us rode across the plateau – our guide leading the way, followed by Frank. As the more experienced rider of the two of us, I brought up the rear. The plateau was a forbidding place, edged on either side by black basalt cliffs. The tops of these cliffs were covered in snow. When the sun set, we kept going. There was a smell of sulphur from the volcanic pools. The smell disturbed the ponies; they began skittering about and had to be steered into the wind.

Soon Frank and the guide were almost invisible. But still we carried on. On either side of me I could hear the mud plopping in the volcanic pools, a sound at once solemn and ridiculous. All at once my pony stopped. I think I must have pulled on the reins without being aware of it. To begin with, I doubted the evidence of my eyes. Only slowly did I allow myself to acknowledge what I was seeing.

An enormous illuminated blanket, the palest green in colour, appeared to have been spread on the ground. On either side, it stretched right to the furthest edges of the plateau, rippling away in impossible, luminous waves. Never before have I experienced such wonder and awe. Yet with it came the strangest feeling of displacement, as if the world had been turned on its head and we were riding our ponies along the bottom of the sea. I tried to hold on to the memory now, hoping that some of the wonder I had felt then might help dispel this gnawing, corrosive sense of emptiness.

The door swung back with a bang. Robert ran in. His shirt was not tucked in properly and his collar was all twisted round.

'There you are, Mama!' he exclaimed.

'Will you please knock before you come in, Robert!' I said. 'How many times have I told you not to run? What on earth is the point of my telling you things if you don't take the slightest notice of what I say?'

Robert stopped immediately.

He looked as if he had been slapped across the face. For several seconds he was unable to say anything. His chest rose and fell with the effort of breathing.

I could still hear my voice, angry and querulous. It continued ringing in my ears as I said, 'Was there anything in particular you wished to see me about, Robbie?'

'Yes – yes, there was . . .' he said.

He paused, apparently unsure whether to go on.

'What is it, then?'

'It's about Mr Brown, Mama.'

'What about Mr Brown?'

'He says he has found something.'

Basil Brown
May–June 1939

All week it kept bucketing down. The rain came in over our boots. It seeped under the tarpaulins and leaked through the roof of the shepherd's hut. The wheelbarrow kept sinking into the ground, right up to the axle. We laid down planks for tracks. The trouble is that the barrow is so heavy when it's fully laden that it's near impossible to steer in a straight line. Also the rain makes the planks slippery, of course. At times it felt as if we were hardly going forward at all. Then, at around three o'clock on Thursday, I was down at the bottom of the trench when I heard John Jacobs shout, 'Baz!'

'What is it?'

'Can you come here?'

I scrambled up the bank to where John was standing. He was holding a piece of iron. It was about four inches in length, much corroded and roughly the shape of a bolt.

When I asked him to show me where he'd found it, he pointed at a pinky-brown patch in the sand. As soon as I saw it, I asked the men to step away. Then I knelt down with my trowel. I was all set to start scraping when I noticed another patch of pink sand. This one was about six inches away, on the left-hand side. Although not as big or clear as the first, it was still clear enough.

I dug down. An inch or so below the patch of sand was a second piece of metal – even more corroded than before, but the same shape. Just like a bolt. I moved along, not scraping now, only looking. Another six inches away from the second patch of sand there was a third one.

Now what have we got here? I thought.

Before going on, I had another look at John's piece of iron. Also at the one I'd just found. I had a strong suspicion that I'd seen them before. Or something very like them anyway. But where and when?

I sat down on the ledge and tried to remember. I was damned if I could dredge anything up. I was close to banging my head with my fist when all at once it popped into my mind: Aldeburgh. Yes, that's it. There's another one of these at Aldeburgh, I was positive there was, although it must have been a good fifteen years since I saw it.

Brushing myself down, I told John and Will that I'd be gone for a few hours and that it was very important they shouldn't disturb anything while I was away. Then I put the pieces of iron into my pocket, climbed on my bike and headed north – towards Orford.

As I rode along, the clouds finally began to lift. By the time I reached Rendlesham Forest the mist was already rising off the trees. Coming closer to the sea, the breeze was so strong it nearly took my cap off. Beyond Orford, I carried on along the coast road. On the right-hand side, the land shelved down to the water. I rode through fields of wheat and sedge, until I reached the ferry crossing opposite Slaughden. As luck would have it, a ferry was waiting there, about to depart. I cycled on and then hung about impatiently for several more minutes while some further dawdling took place.

Slowly, the ferry cast off and inched its way across the river. I spent the crossing astride my bike, staring at the opposite bank, willing it to come closer. The moment the ferry touched land, I was off, pedalling into town, past the boathouses and the beach huts. A couple of people called out to me. One of them – I've no idea who – shouted, 'What's the hurry?' but I didn't stop. I just lifted a hand as I rode past.

I parked my bike outside the museum. There was a woman behind the desk who I didn't recognize. I asked if Mr Brightling was in. Oh, no, she said in a shocked voice, sounding as if he'd either died or emigrated years before. I didn't inquire which. I just explained who I was and asked if I could have a look in their storeroom.

She wasn't at all happy about this. She spent a while wobbling about on the edge of refusing, glancing at her watch and explaining how the museum was due to close in less than half an hour. They did stay open later, she explained – until six, in fact. However, that was only on a Wednesday, which wasn't a great deal of help. Not with this being a Thursday.

'It could be important,' I said. 'Very important.'

Still she wouldn't budge, though. In desperation, I said, 'Mr Reid Moir sent me.'

That did the trick, of course. The change in her was instantaneous. 'Why didn't you say so straight away?' she wanted to know. I muttered something about not wishing to make a fuss. Afterwards, she set about being as helpful as could be, showing me through into the storeroom, apologizing for the mess and offering me a cup of tea.

I turned down the tea and set to looking through the drawers. Although the room was small, there were cabinets stacked up from floor to ceiling on all four walls. There was only just enough room to allow the door to open and shut. She wasn't wrong about the mess. I remembered that old Brightling had never been much of a one for cataloguing. Nor had his successor made much effort to improve matters, not by the look of it. In one drawer alone I found a boxful of Bronze Age arrowheads, three half-hunter watches – one missing the back of its case as well as one of the hands – and a container of Joyce's anti-corrosive percussion gunpowder, along with several packets of mustard seed apparently from the Garden Tomb in Jerusalem.

After half an hour my mouth was dry and I wished I'd accepted that tea. Still, it was too late now. I was crouched down, searching through one of the lower drawers, when I saw a piece of purple cloth. It was all tattered round the edges, with threads coming away. I picked up the cloth and realized it had been rolled round something. Something heavy and cylindrical.

When I unrolled the cloth, there it was. I took out the first piece of iron that I'd found at Sutton Hoo and compared them. The one in the drawer was smaller, but the same shape. Any fool could have seen that. Underneath it was a typed label giving the date of discovery, along with the place where it had been found: May 1870, Snape Common.

I turned the label over. Handwritten on the back was an identification. Or a possible identification at least – whoever had written it had stuck a question mark on the end to cover themselves. I must have stayed staring at the label for several minutes. Trying to take it in and think through the implications. Steady on, Basil, I told myself. Easy does it. But even as I was doing so, I could hear my heart thumping. As for my mouth, it was drier than ever.

Rolling up the piece of iron in the purple cloth, I put it back in the drawer with the label. On my way out, I thanked the woman behind the desk for her help.

'Did you find what you were looking for?' she asked.

'Not sure exactly,' I told her.

'I do hope you haven't had a wasted trip,' she said. 'Do be sure to give my regards to Mr Reid Moir, won't you?'

'Oh, I will,' I promised. 'I will.'

Needless to say the blasted ferry was on the opposite bank when I got back to Slaughden. I had to stand and wait while it idled its way across. On the way back it began spitting with rain again. I cycled as fast as I could. By the time I'd covered the eight miles to Sutton Hoo House I was wheezing away like Puffing Billy.

John and Will were waiting inside the shepherd's hut. Mrs Pretty's boy, Robert, was in there too. I can't say I was best pleased to see him. Right at that moment, I didn't want any distractions.

'Any joy, Baz?' asked Will.

'Come with me, will you, lads,' I said. 'And bring the tape measure.'

We went back outside. Before we started, I remembered to take a note of the time. It was just after five thirty. Next, I knelt down where John had found the first piece of metal. I took the tape measure and measured off six inches to the second patch of coloured sand. Then, carrying on in a straight line, I looked for another pink patch six inches away.

There was nothing. I brushed around to make sure. No, definitely nothing. I couldn't understand this. It must be there, I thought – it has to be. Then I realized I was being an idiot. Naturally they wouldn't be in a straight line. They'd have to widen out as they went along. Of course they would.

Moving half a pace to the left, I tried there. This time, I had to go a little deeper, but soon the pinkish sand began to show through, just like before. Within half an hour I had uncovered five patches of pink sand. All of them were the same distance apart, but spreading out towards the edge of the trench. Each one set a little deeper than the one before.

'What is it?' the boy kept asking. 'What have you found, Mr Brown?'

I didn't want to tell him. But it wasn't just him. I didn't want to tell anybody. Not for a little longer. Once I did, everything would be out in the open. Then there'd be no going back. Besides, I told myself, I needed to uncover one more patch before I could be sure.

Again, I marked off a six-inch gap in the same widening line and scraped away. Sure enough, I hadn't been going long when another smudge of brownish-pink sand started to appear. There beneath it was another piece of metal. This time, though, I left it where it was.

I looked up. The three of them were crowded round, staring down. I could see the boy was bursting to ask another question. Before he could open his mouth, I said, 'I think it's a ship.'

John Jacobs was the first to say anything. 'A ship?' he said. 'How do you mean a ship?'

'A ship that's been buried in the mound.'

He started to laugh. 'What would anyone want to bury a ship for?'

'Probably because it's a grave.'

'Whose grave?'

'I don't know that, not yet. But someone important, I'd say. It must be. They wouldn't have gone to all this trouble for any little squirt. Think of all the work for a start. They'd have had to drag the ship all the way up the slope from the river. That piece of metal you found there, John – that's a rivet. These pink patches show where the other rivets are. See how they've rusted and coloured up the soil.'

'But, Baz, if it's a ship, what's happened to the hull?' asked Will.

'All rotted away,' I said. 'But look here –' and I pointed to where a ridge of hard sand ran from one rivet to the next. 'You can see where the strakes were. They've left this imprint. That's all that's left. That and the rivets.'

All of them wanted to know how old this ship might be. I told them that I couldn't be sure about that either. It might be Viking, I said. Or maybe older still, I added.

'Well, I'll be –' said Will, and pulled himself up short.

I looked up at him and grinned. 'Quite.'

I'd been intending to let Mrs Pretty know what I had found, of course. But Robert must have run back to tell her before I had a chance to do so. One moment he'd been jumping up and down, waving his arms about. The next he was walking along with his mother, tugging away at her sleeve.

When she reached the mound, I showed Mrs Pretty the rivets and the patches of sand. Then I told her about finding the other rivet in Aldeburgh, as well as the note explaining how it had come from the ship-burial at Snape.

71

She inspected the rivet for some time.

Then to my surprise she stuck out her hand. 'Congratulations, Mr Brown,' she said. She paused and, as she did so, the corners of her mouth seemed to drift upwards. 'I always told you I thought there was something in there, didn't I?'

'You certainly did, Mrs Pretty. You certainly did . . .'

She also shook John's hand and Will's. We all stood around for a while, grinning like halfwits. By now it was past seven o'clock and we decided to pack it in for the day. Mrs Pretty and Robert went back to the house. When we had finished covering over the trench with tarpaulins and pieces of hessian, John and Will suggested we go for a drink to celebrate. But I was too fired up to be able to take any company.

Instead, I walked down to the estuary. The cow parsley already came up to my shoulders, while the row of railings that marked out the path was all but buried under brambles. Beating my way through to the water's edge, I sat on the bank with only a few squabbling ducks for company. There were clumps of hairy-stalked nettles, as well as a great expanse of docks with ragged holes torn in them.

A fishing boat with dark red sails made its way upriver. The only sound was the popping of wild broom pods. When I turned round I could see Sutton Hoo House up on the bluff. The light was blazing in its windows. Behind the house a few spindly pines stood out on the horizon. It reminded me of an illustration from one of the Bible Reading Fellowship books I'd had at school.

I wished May could have been sitting there beside me. Then I could have told her what had happened. I would have liked that. As it was, I just had to imagine her being there. I knew she'd be proud, although she probably wouldn't make too much of it. That's not her way. Even so, she's always hoped I might make something of myself.

I stayed on the bank until I was feeling more or less straightened out. Then I went to the Lyonses' cottage and shared some cold lamb and purple sprouting with Billy and his wife, Vera. Before going to bed, I wrote a letter to May – as well as a longer one to Maynard, giving him as detailed an account as possible of what I'd found. I also wrote to the Reverend Harris at Thornden. I felt sure that he'd be interested. By the time I signed off, I was already half-asleep.

Fortunately, the rain held off and the ground soon dried out. While the men shovelled and sieved, I crept along from one patch of pink sand to the next. Rather than carry on driving a trench into the middle of the mound, I decided to go up and over the rivets, coming down on each one from above. That way I should actually be inside the ship, rather than tunnelling through the middle of it. By scooping the earth out of the inside, I hoped to keep the sandy crust of the hull intact.

That was the plan anyway. Not that I didn't have my doubts about it. But to my relief the outline of the ribs was still there, etched into the sand. All I had to do was brush away the loose sand until I reached the hard crust where the wood had been – and then follow the lines along from one rivet to the next.

As I did so, a number of things became more clear. For a start, the ship is lying at a slant. One end is pointing downwards. Perhaps it was put in like this, or else it just sank down at one end over the years. There's no way of telling. From the way the rivets are spreading out – they're in lines of about seven to every three feet – I think we must have hit one end of the ship almost head-on. I still don't know if this is the stern or the bow. I can't say why exactly, but I've an inkling it's the stern.

The deeper I go, the wider the ship becomes. It's plain now that we're up against a far larger thing than anyone suspected. In reply to my letter, Maynard sent me some useful details about the Snape ship-burial. That ship was forty-six feet long, nine feet nine inches in width and four feet in depth. Judging by the width so far, I reckon this one could easily be of similar size. Perhaps even bigger. However, I have kept quiet about this. I haven't even told Mrs Pretty. There doesn't seem any point raising anybody's hopes. Not at this stage.

I've taken to starting work at five in the morning, as soon as there's enough light to see by. First, I smoke a pipe, pace around and have a think before climbing down the ladder into the trench. Due to the dewfall, the stratification in the soil is clearest then. Also, there's nothing to beat the sense of having stolen a march on the day.

At eight o'clock, John and Will arrive. Soon afterwards, depending on the weather, Mrs Pretty and Robert come to watch our progress. As I go along, I point out the rivets and pass up anything I've uncovered. So far, I've found five small pieces of turquoise-blue glass and one glazed ceramic bead, also blue.

It's not much, I know. Less than I would have expected, even at this stage. I can't rule out the possibility that the mound has been robbed. Although the robbers might have started digging in the wrong place, they could have changed direction as they went along. Or they might simply have struck lucky. Still, there's no suggestion yet that the rivets have been disturbed. That must be a good sign, I keep telling myself.

When John and Will have left for the day, I work on alone for another couple of hours. Due to the angle of the light, the discoloured sand shows up especially well at sunset. I can now stand at the entrance of the trench and see lines of pink patches sweeping away before me and then disappearing into the depths of the mound.

Whenever Mrs Pretty stays inside or is driven into Woodbridge, her son comes out on his own. Robert's a nice enough boy, eager as anything and grateful for the company, I suspect. He and Will Spooner have devised a game which they play during our tea breaks. Will has pieces of shrapnel beneath his skin – he picked them up in France when a soldier standing next to him blew himself up with a grenade. Apparently they're not worth the bother of digging out. You can see them in his wrist and on the back of his right hand, dark blue shapes like squashed flies.

For reasons that Will is convinced have to do with the amount of moisture in the air, these pieces of metal move about. Sometimes they're down by his knuckles. An hour later they might have crawled up under his watch strap. Their game involves the boy shutting his eyes and pointing to where he thinks one of the pieces of metal might be. Then he opens them to see if he's right. They can go on like this for ages. He never seems to tire of it.

In order to make him feel useful, I've taught him how to brush the earth away from the rivets. I told him – truthfully enough – that he was being trusted with a very great responsibility and that it was vital he stopped brushing the moment the earth changed colour from yellow to pink. At first, he was so nervous that he could hardly hold the brush. But after just a few days he's become quite a dab hand at it. By way of a reward, I've given him his own trowel. He hangs it on the peg in the hut along with the others.

In order to deter any trespassers, Mrs Pretty suggested we should cordon off the site. She asked me what I thought and I agreed it was a good idea. One evening, Billy Lyons brought stakes, ropes and a sledgehammer. The four of us erected a rough fence around the mound.

When we had finished, Billy hung a sign that he'd written in big white letters from the rope: DANGER! LIVE BOMBS!

'There,' he said. 'That should keep the buggers away.'

All the time I've been waiting for the rivets to spread out to their furthest point, then start narrowing again. But they just keep on getting wider. I'm now twenty-five feet in from the first rivets, as well as nine feet below the original ground level. In order to give ourselves enough room, we've also had to widen the trench. This is now fully forty feet from one side to the other.

There's no doubt now that this ship is bigger than the one at Snape. And by a good way too. The only ship that can compare to it – the only one I'm aware of anyway – is the one found at Oseberg in Norway in 1906. That was more than seventy feet long. Without wanting to jump ahead of myself, ours could end up that big. Which of course would make it the largest ship-burial ever found on English soil.

Whenever I allow myself to think about it, I feel hot and cold at the same time. The hot part's all right – that's just excitement. But for some reason I can't shake this sense of dread that it might all go wrong.

Then, midway through yesterday afternoon, a letter came from Maynard that changed everything. 'I have been doing some research into the objects found in the Snape burial,' he wrote. 'As you know, Basil, the chamber itself was looted. However, a mass of auburn-coloured hair was discovered at one end of it. This was believed to have come from some sort of ceremonial cloak. In addition to the mass of hair, they found fragments of a green glass goblet. This goblet was later identified as being early Anglo-Saxon in style.' He'd underlined the words 'early Anglo-Saxon'.

That really did it, of course. All this time I'd been assuming the Sutton Hoo ship was Viking. I hadn't even allowed myself to go back any further. But if it was Anglo-Saxon? And not just any old Anglo-Saxon, but early Anglo-Saxon? Obviously that threw all my ideas right into the air. Threw them about as high as it was possible to go. Apart from anything else, it made the ship much older than I thought. Up to 300 years older – early Anglo-Saxon meaning anything between the fifth and sixth centuries. That would put it slap bang in the middle of the Dark Ages.

I'd hardly finished taking all this in when Mrs Pretty came to see how we were getting along. In the six weeks I've been at Sutton Hoo, she seems to have become thinner, more gaunt. And to move more stiffly too. That said, though, there's been a bit more of a spring in her step since we found the ship. I told her all about Maynard's letter and about the likely length of her ship.

While I was explaining about the goblet, I thought I saw her starting to sway. I reached out to steady her, but she held up her hand to stop me.

'Shall I go on?' I asked.

'Please, Mr Brown.'

When I had finished, I fetched two chairs from the hut. Then we sat down under the yew trees. Partly to stop my own head from becoming too mazy, I talked about the Oseberg dig. As I recall, the burial chamber there was in the centre of the ship. From the outside, it had appeared intact. Inside, though, beds, carts and even a sleigh had been found, all jumbled together.

It turned out that grave-robbers had looted the valuables by cutting a hole in the chamber roof and then lowering someone – a child most probably – down on a rope. I told Mrs Pretty that I'd write back to Maynard to see if there was any other information he could find.

She was about to leave when she said there was something that she'd been meaning to tell me. Something that had slipped her mind in all the excitement. Apparently a lot of people had said how they would like to see the ship. Word having got round, as it does. She'd decided that the best way to accommodate them all would be to hold a sherry party one evening and invite anyone who was interested.

Perhaps I might give a brief talk, Mrs Pretty wondered. Explain what was going on and so forth. How would I feel about that?

I need hardly say it was just about the last thing I wanted. Having people clumping about, churning up the ground and asking a lot of damn-fool questions. On the other hand, of course, I was in no position to object.

'That sounds a very good idea,' I said.

'Excellent. In which case I shall have the invitations printed.' Then she said, 'I also wanted to thank you, Mr Brown.'

'Thank me Mrs Pretty?'

'For being so patient with Robert.'

'Oh, we don't mind him a bit. Keeps us on our toes, it does, having him around.'

'I know it means a great deal to him. He can hardly wait to come out and see you every morning. Do you and your wife have any children, Mr Brown?'

'No,' I said. 'No, we don't. We would have liked to have done – May especially. Somehow it just never happened, though.'

'I'm sorry. I had no wish to pry.'

'No, no. That's quite all right.'

'And how are you finding the work, Mr Brown? Are you sure you can manage on your own? I would not want you overdoing it.'

'Don't you worry about me, Mrs Pretty,' I told her. 'I'm a tough old bird. Takes a lot to ruffle my feathers.'

She looked at me from under the brim of her hat. 'Yes,' she said. 'I would imagine that it does.'

There was a letter from May waiting for me at the cottage. Her writing was even more of a scramble than usual. It was also spattered with trails of ink blots.

My dear Basil,

I had a great shock last night. Mr Potter was staying at Diss and came over. I think he was after putting rent up as he said the rates had gone up another 6d a week and he wondered if I could help I told him I could not afford any more. I told him lot wanted doing I had never had anything done copper and cooking stove were no good. I expect I shall get a letter before rent day more rent or notice. We have been here just 4 years and only had a lavatory pail. I

*was quite nice to him and polite. We had dreadful thunder
storms in the night one of the apple trees was struck by
lightning. The branches are still smoking I can see them
from the bedroom window. I hope you get a good job after
this but I don't suppose you will. Best love my dear best of
luck in your digging you take care of your dear self looking
forward to seeing you.*

    Yours always
    May

I put her letter in the bedside drawer, along with all the
others she'd sent. I'd been intending to write back to her, to
tell her what had happened. However, I was so tired I fell
fast asleep in my clothes.

I sat up in the middle of the night, unable at first to work
out what had woken me. It didn't take long, though. Rain
was drumming against the window, coming down so hard
it sounded as if someone was chucking pebbles at the glass.
Fetching a torch, I made my way downstairs. There was an
oilskin hanging by the door. I pulled it over my head.

Outside, the rain was blowing near horizontal. As I ran
towards the mounds, gusts battered against my chest.
Pushing me back. Once there, I saw it was just as I had
feared. The wind had uprooted the tarpaulins. They were
cracking and flapping about like untethered sails.

Rain was pouring into the ship. I fetched a mallet from
the shepherd's hut, knocking over the kettle in the process,
then slipping on the steps as I came down. It was hard to
know where to start. When I grabbed hold of one of the
tarpaulins, immediately it pulled me over. I tried again, but
the same thing happened.

But this time I was able to thrash about with my feet and elbows and gain some purchase. From there, it was possible to pull the tarpaulin towards me. With one hand I kept it taut while stretching out the ropes and hammering in the pegs. Once I had this secure, I tried to throw the ropes from one side of the ship to the other – only to have the rope come slapping back into my face.

The only solution was to tie two pieces of rope together. Then I dragged them round the exposed end of the ship – this before stretching out the tarpaulin and securing the other side. I managed to secure the first two pegs. But on the third I lost my footing again and began sliding down the bank, right into the innards of the ship.

I dug my fingers in. I could feel wet sand raking through them, bending my nails back. Finally I came to a halt. First, I threw one arm forward, then the other. Hand over hand, I began to haul myself up the bank, not daring to use my feet in case I caused any more damage. When I reached the top of the bank I could see the tree tops tossing about above my head. For a moment or two I just lay there with the rain falling on my face. Quickly, I pulled myself together. Still on all fours, I scuttled from one tarpaulin to the next, tugging and hammering away until I had secured them all.

Even when all the tarpaulins were pegged back down, ripples of air swept back and forth beneath them, puffing out the material. I had no idea how much water had got in. It was impossible to tell until morning came and the sand started to dry out. My biggest worry – I could hardly even bear to think of it – was that a large section of the ship might have been completely washed away.

After cleaning myself off as best as I could, I headed back

to the cottage. As the path rounded the bend near Sutton Hoo House, I saw there was a light on upstairs. The curtains were half-drawn. In the gap between them stood the silhouette of a figure, staring out into the night.

The moment dawn broke, I was up and out of the house. All the way to the mounds I kept dreading what I might find. First, I unpegged the tarpaulins and rolled them back. Then I looked inside. I had to have another look to make sure. As far as I could tell, there was no damage at all. In fact, there was scarcely evidence of any rainfall – apart from a general darkening of the soil. For a moment I even wondered if I'd imagined the whole thing.

I spent the next hour and a half waiting for John and Will to arrive, growing increasingly impatient and wondering what could be keeping them – until I remembered that it was a Saturday and they wouldn't be coming at all.

However, the boy Robert did come out to help. I gave him a broom and we spent the next hour or so sweeping away the puddles of water from around the edges of the tarpaulins. When we had finished I said, 'Time for some tea, don't you think?'

'Yes, please.'

We went into the hut and I boiled the kettle on the Primus stove. I spooned the tea from the caddy into the pot and then poured in the water. Steam rose and gathered under the roof. I held the mug cupped in my hands. As I did so, I noticed the boy held his mug the same way. While we were waiting for the tea to cool, he said, 'Do you know who built your ship, Mr Brown?'

'Not exactly, no. Not yet. I thought at first it was the

Vikings. But now it looks as if it was the Anglo-Saxons. The Vikings, they didn't invade until about AD 900. But if it's the Anglo-Saxons that would make it older. Much older,' I added.

He thought about this, then said, 'But there's something I don't understand.'

'What's that?'

'Why anyone would want to bury a ship under the ground.'

'Probably so that the ship could take whoever was buried inside from this world into the next.'

'But where is this next world, Mr Brown?'

'Ah, well. No one is absolutely sure about that.'

'How do they know it's there if nobody is sure?'

'They don't know. Not exactly. They just . . . hope.'

'But surely they should have some idea?'

'I suppose they should really. I can't say I've ever thought about it like that before.'

'I mean, I know where Norwich is, even though I've never been there.'

'It's more complicated than that,' I told him.

'How?'

'Because it just is. It's something you'll understand better when you're older.'

He went back to staring at his tea. But not for long. He looked up and seemed about to speak. Then he stopped himself.

'Go on, boy.'

'Do you think there will be a war, Mr Brown?'

'I don't know. I hope not.'

'Mr Grateley thinks there will be. So does Mr Lyons.'

'Do they now?'

I took out my pipe and began cleaning it. Running my

penknife round the inside of the bowl and then tapping it on the wall of the hut to dislodge the bits and pieces.

'What was it like?' he asked.

'What was what like?'

'Fighting.'

I filled the pipe with a wad of tobacco and lit it. Smoke drifted up in front of my face.

'I didn't fight,' I said.

'You didn't fight?' he repeated, his voice rising in astonishment.

'No.'

'Why ever not?'

'Because they wouldn't have me. They reckoned I wasn't medically fit. On account of an illness I had when I was about your age.'

'What sort of illness.'

'Diphtheria.'

'Oh . . . Mr Spooner and Mr Jacobs both fought.'

'Yes, I know they did.'

'Were you very sad about not being able to fight?'

'Yes, I was.'

'Most of your friends must have gone.'

I nodded.

'Did many of them die?'

'Sixty-one men from my village alone.'

Now we both sat and stared down at our tea. Strips of grass showed through the gaps in the floor – greener than usual for being so thin.

'If the Germans do invade, Mr Brown, do you think they will sail up the estuary and land at Woodbridge?'

I laughed and said, 'I don't think there's much chance of that.'

'They might do, you know.'

'Why do you say that?'

'Because it's been done before.'

'Who by?' I said, humouring him.

'By the Vikings.'

He was quite right, of course, although I'd never thought of it before. I must have been too stuck in the past to join it up to the present. Now that it had been, I couldn't help wishing it had stayed where it was.

'Come on, then,' I said. 'We can't stay here nattering all day.'

I threw the dregs of my tea through the door. Robert followed my example. However, he had more tea left in his mug than I did and it splashed over my boots.

By the time we came out, I reckoned it was safe to climb down the ladder into the ship. Even at close quarters there didn't seem to be any serious damage. Nothing but a few minor slippages. The ribs of sand were still quite hard and the pink patches were showing up just as clearly as before. I'd been toying with the idea of making a start on the centre of the ship. But without Will and John to help shift the earth, there wasn't much I could do on my own.

The next best thing seemed to be to carry on round the sides. It wasn't long before I found something that made my heart sink – signs of a filled-in hole. It descended straight from the middle of the barrow, right to where the burial chamber might be. The remains of the robbers' flute. You could see the change in the soil quite clearly. It was like a chimney dropping down into the ground.

So they'd been here all right. Just as I feared. However, it was impossible to tell at this stage if the hole extended all the way into the ship or stopped short. At one side of it were the remains of a burnt-off post. There was a central core of black surrounded by a red ash band. I reckoned this was probably the remains of a fire that had been lit by the robbers. My suspicions were confirmed by some shards of pottery that I found close by. These weren't Anglo-Saxon – nothing like it. More like sixteenth century, I'd say.

When I had finished trowelling and brushing, the post jutted up eight inches in the air – a good deal narrower round the base than it was round the top. As I was clearing away the last of the sand, I looked up to see Reid Moir framed against the sky.

'There you are, Brown,' he said, as if this was the last place in the world he expected to find me.

He showed no sign of wanting to come down the ladder. Probably he was bothered about muddying his clothes. Instead, he waited at the top for me to join him.

'So, this is it, then?' he said when I'd done so.

'This is it,' I confirmed.

He nodded, his head moving smoothly up and down like a pump handle.

'Bigger than Snape, then?'

'Oh, yes. Bigger than Snape. Definitely.'

'And Oseberg?'

'Still too early to say.'

'Hmm . . . You realize what this means, don't you? We – Ipswich, that is – will be the envy of every museum in the country. In Europe even. Just think of that.'

'I know,' I said. 'I have been.'

He gave a smile of sorts. 'Now then, Brown, I hope you haven't gone around telling anyone about anything.'

'How do you mean, Mr Reid Moir?'

'I mean, I hope you haven't told anyone what has been discovered here.'

'No,' I said. 'No, I don't think so.'

'Good. That's a relief.'

'Except for my wife.'

'Oh . . .' he said. 'Your wife? Can she be trusted to keep quiet?'

'I would have thought so. To be honest, she's not that interested in archaeology.'

'So much the better. The last thing we want is anyone else sniffing about and trying to steal our thunder.'

I thought Reid Moir might have finished. But I was wrong. 'I assume you have been keeping a field book. With everything properly detailed. Sketched, measured and so forth?'

'Of course.'

'Show it to me, please?'

I fetched the field book from the shepherd's hut. Reid Moir started to leaf through the pages. Slowly at first and then more quickly. And then he stopped. With the book still open in his hands, he looked up.

'But, Brown, this is the most frightful mess. I mean, just look at these drawings. They're desperately crude. And some of the entries are in pencil. Don't you realize this could be an important document? One that reflects on everyone concerned with the excavation. Just think, man. Surely I don't need to remind you who you are working for.'

'For Mrs Pretty,' I said.

'What? No, no . . . Now don't bandy semantics with me, Brown. You know perfectly well what I am talking about. You must make more of an effort with your presentation. I hardly need point out that we are in a very delicate position here. The last thing we want is criticism from other quarters.'

Closing the book and handing it back to me, he said, 'I also notice you appear to have a child working here.'

I explained that Robert was Mrs Pretty's son.

'I see . . . None the less, it creates a sloppy impression. Try to ensure he is less visible in future, will you?'

For the rest of the day I carried on smarting over Reid Moir's comments. I was so angry I even stopped work early. When I arrived back at the cottage there was a parcel from Maynard. Inside it was a large green-bound volume and a letter explaining that this was the only information he had been able to find on the Oseberg dig. I looked at the account of the excavation. It certainly seemed thorough, and there were plenty of illustrations. Unfortunately, it was in Norwegian.

I wrote to May, saying that in future I will pack it in and go home rather than be dictated to. That evening at supper, I dare say I was a bit quieter than usual. By way of making conversation, Billy asked me if I had ever heard the story of Colonel and Mrs Pretty's courtship.

'No,' I told him. 'I don't believe I have.'

'It's quite a tale,' he said. 'Isn't it, Vera?'

Vera agreed that it was quite a tale. With no further encouragement Billy was off, with Vera making appropriate noises in all the right places. Apparently Colonel Pretty had lived up in Lancashire, close to Mrs Pretty's family – or Miss Edith Dempster, as she was then. The Dempsters had made their money from building gasometers. Miss Edith was an only child. Her mother had died when she was young and she had stayed on at home, looking after her father. He'd been in poor health – although Billy didn't know with what.

Every Sunday, the colonel used to see Miss Edith in church. When her father's health permitted, he would pay her a visit. And then, on her eighteenth birthday, the colonel asked Miss Edith to marry him. However, she turned him down, saying she couldn't possibly leave her father on his own. The following year he proposed again – also on her birthday. Once again she said no.

The colonel, though, was nothing if not perseverant. The next year he was back again. And the next. But still the same thing happened. Every year he would come – always on Miss Edith's birthday – and every year she would turn him down. This went on for seventeen years.

'Seventeen years!' repeated Vera in a dreamy sort of way. This while looking over at me to make sure I'd taken it in.

Finally, the old boy had died. When the colonel came round next year, he made his proposal. And this time she said yes, she would marry him. But by now she was in her mid-thirties. As for the colonel, he was over fifty. None the less, they married and moved down here to make a fresh start. They were here for about ten years. And then something quite unexpected happened. At the age of forty-seven, Mrs Pretty fell pregnant.

'Forty-seven!' repeated Vera again. Except this time I nearly beat her to it. Before supper I'd been so angry I couldn't concentrate on anything else. But now all that had disappeared. For the first time in a long while I wasn't thinking about the ship. Apart from anything else, I'd never heard of anyone that age having a child.

At first there were no problems, Billy said. But then midway through her term Mrs Pretty had caught typhus.

Although the baby – Robert – was fine, her health had never recovered. Not fully. As for the colonel, he had died of a heart attack in the spring of 1937. Died on his birthday by an odd sort of coincidence.

None of us said too much afterwards. When I went up to bed, I found I couldn't sleep. Not for a while anyway. I couldn't get this picture of the colonel out of my mind. Every time I shut my eyes I saw him climbing up these stone steps to a big front door – and then going back down again. I wondered how he'd stood it. Year after year of being turned down. All the time hoping that one day his luck might change.

I woke just after four o'clock. Lying in bed, I waited for the sky to lighten. Eventually dawn broke with an angry flourish. As I walked out to the mounds, purple bands spread themselves across the horizon. The water in the estuary was all ruffled up with a mass of white-crested waves rushing this way and that.

As the morning went on, my spirits began to lift. I became convinced that the grave-robbers never reached the burial in the Sutton Hoo ship. They tried – obviously – but stopped short for some reason. I'd dug out around four feet of the flute when it just dwindled away. Underneath it, the soil was all thick and sticky again. Perhaps they were frightened of being buried, or maybe they just became disheartened.

I explained to John and Will that from now on we would be concentrating on the middle of the ship, rather than following the lines of the rivets. They didn't see anything unusual in this. Or if they did they were too tactful to say so.

Once again, I proposed working down in layers from the

surface. First moving in one direction, then coming back in the other, taking off about six inches at a time. With our coal shovels attached to the ends of long ash handles, we began shaving down the area. These ash handles come in very handy, allowing us to toss the earth right out of the trench to be barrowed off.

All day, we continued shaving away, keeping a careful watch for any changes in the colour of the sand. It was while John and I were working on the section west of the centre of the ship – Will was on wheelbarrow duty at the time, with Robert helping out – that I came across a darkened discoloration. It was no more than quarter of an inch wide, running crossways across the ship. First of all I took it to be the remains of another of the rib timbers. But the more I thought, the less sure I was. It could be another of the timbers, of course. On the other hand, it could be all that was left of one of the walls of the chamber itself.

Unfortunately there was no time left to do anything about it. John and Will knocked off at six and an hour or so later Robert went in for his supper. Instead of carrying on, I wanted to have another think while I decided what to do next. I'd already unfolded the tarps and was preparing to spread them out, when I turned around to see a large, unfamiliar-looking man. He was climbing down the ladder right into the belly of the ship.

'Excuse me!' I called out.

This had no effect, none at all. Although the man could hardly have failed to hear me, he took no notice. Meanwhile, the ladder bowed beneath his weight. As he neared the bottom, I saw that he wasn't simply large around the middle. He was large all over. His trousers were hitched very high over his chest and he wore a spotted bow tie.

'Stop there!' I shouted, much more loudly than before.

At this, he finally came to a halt.

'What do you think you're doing?'

He looked straight through me. Or rather over my shoulder at the lines of rivets running off into the sand.

'Ye gods,' he said.

And then he carried on coming down the ladder.

'No, no! You can't!'

Once again he stopped.

'I beg your pardon?' he said, saying it in such a way as to imply that no begging was involved.

'You can't come down here.'

'Why not?'

'Because it's not safe for someone of your –'

'Of my what?'

'Of your build,' I said.

By now he was only two or three rungs from the bottom. In the same slow, deliberate manner as before, he finished climbing down. Having reached the bottom, he stepped on to one of the planks and thrust his chest out at me. He did so like he was presenting it for inspection.

'Megaw said nothing this big had ever been found before. Certainly not in East Englia –' that was how he pronounced it. 'Even so, I never expected this.'

I'd had enough by now. 'Look here,' I said, 'I've asked you twice to leave. That should be enough for anyone, but I'm doing so again. This is a very delicate site. And a dangerous one,' I said, pointing up at Billy's LIVE BOMBS! sign.

'What about the chamber?' he asked.

'Chamber? What chamber?'

'Have you found any sign of the burial chamber?'

92

Perhaps he was out of breath, but when he spoke to me he broke up his words into pieces as if he was talking to a child.

'No,' I said. 'Nothing.'

Shortly afterwards, he started to climb back up the ladder. Halfway up, though, he stopped and gazed back down at the ship.

'Ye gods,' he said again.

When I returned to the cottage Vera said, 'There's a surprise waiting upstairs for you, Basil.'

I can't say I was in any mood for more surprises. 'What do you mean?'

She laughed. 'You go and have a look for yourself.'

May was standing in my bedroom. There were red patches on her cheeks. Around the brim of her bonnet her hair was sticking out all over the place.

'What are you doing here?' I asked.

'Old Middleton was coming into Woodbridge. He offered me a lift. You sounded so out of sorts in your last letter, Basil, that I was worried. I thought I'd better see how you were. And I've brought you some fresh clothes.'

'I'm all right,' I said. 'I am now anyway.'

'Really?'

She lifted her chin and I gave her a kiss. Then we sat together on the bed. The bed is a metal-framed affair, set unusually high off the ground. So high that our legs hung off the sides. The sun was shining straight in through the window. We both had to shield our eyes from the glare.

'Are you pleased to see me, Basil?'

'Course I am.'

'You don't show it much,' she said.

I gave her another kiss. When we'd finished, I said, 'Why don't you take your hat off?'

She pulled out the pins. As she lifted the hat, her hair sprang up all round her head in stiff corkscrews. 'There, is that better?'

'Much better – even better,' I added quickly.

'That Reid Moir. Behaving like he's Lord God Almighty. If I ever see him I'd like to give him a piece of my mind.'

'Luckily there's not much chance of that.'

'You're too trusting, Basil. Yes, you are. How big did you say this ship of yours is?'

'Sixty-four feet so far.'

'Sixty-four feet!'

'And I reckon there could easily be another fifteen to go.'

'Something like this, everyone's going to want a part of it. You'll need to watch your back.'

'I'll be all right.'

'No, really, Basil. I mean it. Play this one properly and you could make quite a name for yourself.'

'I'll be all right,' I said again, quite keen to change the subject. 'So what happened with Potter and the rent?'

'He's not come back. I think I saw him off. For the time being at least.'

'I hope so.'

'The cheek of it, really. Seeing how little he's done for us.'

'Best keep him sweet,' I said.

'Don't you go worrying, Basil.'

'Nothing we can do anyway, is there?'

'Nothing at all.'

The sun was sinking now, just a last few shafts coming in through the window. Downstairs, Billy and Vera were talking. I could hear the mumble of their voices coming up through the floorboards.

'What else have you been up to, then?'

'Nothing much,' she said. 'This and that . . .'

Something about May's voice made me ask, 'What do you mean, "This and that?"'

'Nothing!'

'Tell me,' I said.

Her cheeks had turned even redder now. 'I cleared out your books, Basil.'

'You did what?'

'I had to! I could hardly move. Let alone sit down.'

'What have you done with them?'

'I put some in the roof and others in the shed. The rest I stacked in piles. Don't be angry with me.'

'I'm not angry,' I said, and almost meant it.

May pressed down in the middle of the bed.

'I don't think much of this mattress,' she said. 'It's a bit soft, isn't it? Especially here.'

'It does me well enough.'

She brushed her hand over the crocheted bedspread. 'Does this remind you of anything, Basil?'

I laughed. 'Course it does.'

Back when May and I were courting, we arranged to meet one evening on Rickinghall Common. We were going to catch the bus into Stowmarket to see the pictures. May had knitted a dress specially. It was in the latest fashion, just over the knee. But on the way there she had to walk across a hay field. The grass was wet and the moisture weighed down the wool. By the time she reached the common the dress was flapping round her ankles.

'What must I have looked like?'

'I didn't complain, did I?'

'That dress, I don't know what happened to it.'

'You probably cleared it out,' I said.

We sat on the bed as the light faded around us. The dusk was thickening. The air might have been rubbed with charcoal.

'How much longer do you think you'll be here, Basil?'

'Could be another three weeks. A month even.'

'That long! I miss you when you're not at home. Especially now.'

'Come here,' I said.

'I am here, aren't I?'

'Closer.'

She shifted along the mattress towards me. I started rubbing her back. I could feel her bones poking through like buttons. Then I put my hand around her shoulder.

All at once she pulled away. 'Oh, Basil, I can't.'

'What do you mean?'

'Old Middleton said I had to be down at the Orford road at nine if I wanted a lift back.'

'But I don't want you to go.'

'I don't want to go either, Basil. But you know how it is.'

She stood up and started pinning her hat back on. After a while I stood up too. When she'd finished with her hat, she bent over and checked herself in the mirror.

'You be careful with old Middleton,' I told her.

'What do you mean?'

'You heard me.'

'Don't be daft, Basil. They don't call him old Middleton for nothing, you know. Why, you're not jealous, are you?'

'No,' I said. 'Maybe. Just a little.'

'Really, you do talk some rubbish sometimes, you know.'

'Do I?'

'Not that I mind, not necessarily. Makes a girl feel wanted.'

'You should do,' I said.

'Should do what?'

'Feel wanted.'

She laughed. Then she put the backs of her fingers up against my cheek. 'You be sure to take care of yourself.'

'I will.'

'Don't work too hard either. And remember, Basil, don't you take any more nonsense from that Reid Moir.'

The next morning I finished uncovering the line of discoloured sand I'd found the day before. It ran straight across the ship – almost from one gunwale to the other. An hour later, John Jacobs found another one. Again, there was a single discoloured line running across the ship. This second line, though, was less regular than the first – it was more like a faint thread running through the earth.

We measured the gap between the two lines. It was eighteen feet. The more I thought about it, the more likely I reckoned these were the remains of the burial-chamber walls. When I told Mrs Pretty, she insisted on having a look for herself. I held the bottom of the ladder with my foot so that it didn't slide and guided her down rung by rung. She knelt on a piece of hessian and inspected both of the lines.

'You really think this might be it, Mr Brown?'

'I don't know,' I told her. 'Not for sure. But it might be, yes.'

Throughout the afternoon we continued shaving down the area in the centre of the ship, taking it off one thin layer at a time. As we were doing so, I found a third discoloured line. This one was much shorter than the others – barely four feet in length and running downwards as well as outwards towards the position of the gunwale.

Sitting on the edge of the trench, I tried to work out what these lines could mean. The best theory I could fix on was this: the original burial chamber probably sat in the bottom of the ship with a pitched roof, much like a picture of Noah's Ark in a child's storybook. The Oseberg chamber seems to have been built like this – as far as I could tell from the illustrations in Maynard's book. But at some stage the roof must have fallen in. Most likely due to the weight of soil. The fall seems certain to have dislodged the contents of the chamber. Of course, there's also a possibility it might have crushed them in the process.

I drew a sketch of how the chamber might have looked – as close to scale as I could make it. I was staring at this sketch when Maynard appeared. I could tell straight away there was something wrong. He's a real worry-guts at the best of times. Now, though, he looked more bilious than ever. Rather than ask what the matter was, I decided to wait until he told me. As expected, it didn't take long.

'Basil,' he said, 'I fear I have done a foolish thing.'

'How's that, then?'

'I meant no harm by it, I swear. Quite the reverse. My intention was solely to make sure that we – that you were on the right track. I wrote to Megaw in the Isle of Man.'

'Megaw?'

'Yes, at the museum there. I knew that he had records of burials that had been found on the island. Records that could be very useful in determining the precise date of this ship. Well,' he said in a shriller voice than before, 'how could I know that he had been at Cambridge with Charles Phillips? No sooner had Megaw received my letter than he contacted Phillips and read it out to him. Over the telephone,' he added, as if this made the whole thing even worse. 'Now everyone seems to know about the dig. There's already talk of the British Museum becoming involved. And the Ministry of Works.'

'Oh, Lord.'

'I know, Basil. I know . . . I never imagined a little thing would have such implications. As you can imagine, Reid Moir is furious. Apart from anything else, he can't stand Phillips. It turns out there's bad blood between them from way back. Apparently Phillips wrested control of the East Anglia Society from him in the most underhand fashion. You know how Reid Moir can be sometimes – far from reasonable, frankly. He spoke to me in the most – the most disparaging tones.'

I folded up the drawing and put it in my pocket. Maynard was still standing there, looking as if he'd swallowed a pound of worms.

'What do you think we should do, Basil?' he asked.

'Not much we can do, I wouldn't have thought. Except wait and see. Whatever happens, I dare say we'll be the last to know.'

When Robert appeared the next morning, he said that his mother wasn't feeling well and might not come out today. Not unless we found anything significant. He also mentioned that she'd had a visitor the night before. He'd been about to go to bed, he said, when someone had rung the front doorbell.

I can't say I'd been paying much attention to this. Not until Robert said that this visitor had been large. Then I did come to.

'How do you mean "large"?' I asked him.

'Fat,' he said, and giggled. 'Although I'm not meant to say that.'

'What did he look like?'

'I've just told you, Mr Brown.'

'Did you notice anything else about him?'

'He wore a bow tie.'

'Did he now?'

'It had spots on it.'

'Yes,' I said, 'I thought it might have done. And had you seen this man before?'

He shook his head. 'But Mama must have known him.'

'How do you work that out?'

'Because he called her his dear lady.'

'His "dear lady"? How did she like that?'

'I think she pretended not to notice.'

'You didn't happen to catch this man's name, did you?'

'I'm sorry, Mr Brown.'

'Doesn't matter,' I said. 'Doesn't matter at all.'

'But Mr Grateley would know it,' he added. 'He showed him in.'

'So he would.'

'I could run and ask him if you like.'

'No need to do that.'

'Shall I, Mr Brown?'

'Go on, then, boy.'

He ran off, returning just a few minutes later. 'Grateley said that he was called Phillips – Mr Charles Phillips. Do you know him?'

'I know of him. He's an archaeologist. From Selwyn College, Cambridge.'

'What do you think he's doing here?'

'I'm not sure exactly. Although I reckon I can make a pretty good guess.'

Throughout the morning, we kept on digging in the middle of the ship – in the area where I suspected the burial chamber must be. For fear of disturbing the soil, I switched to a trowel, a brush and the bodkin. While this was sure to take longer, there was less risk of doing any damage. Yet despite being careful not to hurry, I felt more of a sense of urgency than ever before. It was like having a metal band round my head, growing tighter and tighter.

Meanwhile, I crept along, scraping and brushing. The three discoloured lines went down a good fourteen inches without getting any lighter. Despite not finding anything, I could be sure of one thing – there were no signs of disturbance. That didn't mean that the burial chamber was still intact, of course. On the other hand, it was hard to see how else any robbers could have got in. Not without leaving a trace. And if the chamber really hadn't been touched – well, anyone with any degree of curiosity would have to wonder what might be inside. No matter how hard they tried to stop themselves.

At the end of the day, when Robert and I had finished covering over the centre of the ship, he said, 'Mr Brown . . .'

'Yes?'

'I've been thinking.'

'You'll give yourself a headache if you're not careful. What have you been thinking about now?'

'If Mama has any more visitors, would you like me to keep my ears open and tell you what happens?'

'Oh, I don't know about that,' I said.

'It wouldn't be any trouble for me.'

'I'm sure it wouldn't. But even so . . .'

'I wouldn't tell anyone either. It could be our secret.'

'Our secret, eh?'

'All I'd have to do was listen.'

'Listeners hear no good of themselves. That's what they say, you know.'

There's a bruised look that comes into Robert's eyes sometimes. When he doesn't understand what's going on, or feels left out.

'All right, then,' I said. 'Our secret. But just make sure you don't get caught.'

'I won't, Mr Brown,' he said – he'd already started running back to the house. 'I promise you.'

There was no sign of Mrs Pretty the following day. I assumed that this was because she was still feeling poorly, but then Robert said she'd gone down to London. He seemed puzzled by this and when I asked why, he said that she normally went on a Wednesday and this was a Thursday.

He also had more information to pass on. The previous evening his mother had had a telephone call from the Ministry of Works. Apparently, they'd been making a lot of fuss about a roof, saying how an excavation of this importance shouldn't be left open to the elements.

Already I could smell the busybodies gathering. Building a roof was bound to take several days, I would have thought – and no doubt all digging would have to be halted in the meantime. Mrs Pretty, however, had not taken kindly to this suggestion. According to Robert, she'd told them to get lost. Or words to that effect anyway.

'She was very angry,' he said. 'I could hear her talking on the telephone from my bedroom. And she was still angry when she came up to read to me. Afterwards, Mama went back downstairs to the sitting room and shut the door behind her . . . I'm afraid that's all I was able to find out.'

'You've done well,' I told him.

'Have I?'

'Yes, you have, boy.'

Putting all this aside, as much as I was able to, I began to excavate the western end of the chamber. Within a few minutes, I came across something solid. Working outwards, I found the edge of this object and began to trowel my way around the outside. After a couple of hours, I could see that the object appeared to be made out of clay. It was about three feet in length and eighteen inches wide. There was a dip in the middle. In this dip I found a number of stones and two small fragments of charcoal.

'Ever seen one of those before, Baz?' John asked after we'd cleaned it off.

I shook my head.

It was a big slab of clay. There was no telling if it had been made by hand. From where it was lying, it must originally have been placed on the roof of the chamber. Somehow the slab had remained in one piece when the roof collapsed.

The four of us prised it free. It was surprisingly light – much lighter than the butcher's tray in the first mound. Underneath lay a square patch of earth. This patch was much darker than the sandy soil all around. Just like a trapdoor.

None of us said anything. We just stared down at the square of darkened earth. As we did so, that sense I'd had of a metal band tightening round my head – all of a sudden it was as if it had sprung apart and wasn't there any more.

'Baz?' said Will quietly.

'Yes,' I said. 'I think so . . .'

Taking the bodkin, I began scratching away. I scratched my way up one narrow strip of earth and then down again. The first chink was so faint I scarcely heard it. I tried again. There was another chink. With the brush, I swept the earth away. As I did so, a bluish-grey shape began to appear.

I told myself it was probably a pebble. I went on telling myself it was a pebble until I could be certain that it wasn't. It was a coin, no bigger than a shirt button. Not entirely circular, but close enough and with sharp edges. I rubbed it down, cleaning off the earth. On one side of it was a plain cross. On the other what appeared to be the imprint of a head.

Everyone crowded round, keen to have a look. When we'd all finished doing so, I looked up to see Grateley walking towards us. His tail coat was swinging behind him.

He stopped at the entrance to the trench. 'I have a message for you, Basil,' he said.

'What's that, then?'

'It's from Mr Charles Phillips.'

'Yes?'

'He says you are to stop work immediately and to replace all the tarpaulins.'

'Stop work?' said John Jacobs. 'What the hell do you mean "stop work"?'

'I'm just passing on what I've been told,' said Grateley. 'All of you are to stop work, with immediate effect.'

'What does this mean, Baz?' Will asked.

'I don't know. Is Mrs Pretty back yet?'

'I am afraid not,' said Grateley. 'Nor do I know when she will return. I am assuming this evening. Unfortunately, she didn't leave a number where we can reach her.'

'May I use the telephone?'

'I already told you, Basil. She can't be contacted.'

'May I use the telephone?' I said again.

Grateley hesitated, far from taken with the idea. Then he said, 'If you think you really need to.'

In the event all of us trooped in through the back door and down the corridor. The telephone was mounted on the wall by the kitchen door. I picked it up and dialled Maynard's number. He answered after the second ring. I explained what had happened. However, it turned out Maynard knew about it already. He said that Reid Moir had had a conversation with Phillips earlier that day. Not that Maynard knew what the conversation had been about – only that Reid Moir was currently trying to reach the relevant person in the Ministry of Works.

'I think it's this business with a roof, Basil,' he said.

'You're telling me we're having to stop for a – for a blasted roof? What ruddy fool came up with that idea?'

I knew I was shouting – I couldn't help it.

'Apparently in exceptional circumstances the ministry can order the landowner to follow their instructions,' said Maynard. 'I believe the ministry has been liaising closely with the British Museum. I also understand there may be other complications.'

'Complications? What other complications?'

'I don't know yet, Basil. Everything is a little fraught here. As I say, I haven't been able to speak to Reid Moir. I think all you can do is wait for Mrs Pretty to come back and then discuss the matter with her.'

'So, you're saying we really do have to stop?'

There was no reply, not at first. I thought we must have been disconnected. And then Maynard came through again. 'I'm sorry, Basil. I don't think you have any choice. I'll do my best to keep you posted. Goodbye.'

There was a click as he put down the receiver. A moment or two later, I did the same.

My first instinct was to write to May and tell her what had happened. Except that I couldn't face putting my thoughts into words. I couldn't face talking to anyone either. After we'd replaced the tarpaulins, I decided to walk into Woodbridge. Just to give myself something to do.

There was hardly any traffic on the road. Only a few cars and a couple of carts – one of them carrying beet, the other piles of hurdles. A boy was spread-eagled on top of the hurdles, clinging on as the load swayed about underneath him. It took me about an hour to reach town. Once there, I headed for the dock and sat on a bench beside the tide mill. I thought that gazing at the river might settle my mind. But it didn't do that at all – it just made me feel like jumping in.

Next, I walked along the High Street, trying to summon some interest in what I saw in the shop windows: the rows of shoes, the shelves of dry goods, the mounds of bric-à-brac behind screens of orange cellophane. The library was already shut so that was no good. I could have gone into a pub, I suppose, but I didn't fancy that either.

And so I carried on aimlessly wandering. Up past the Bull Hotel and St Mary's Church, then veering down the side streets to the right. When I reached the common on the edge of town, I doubled back, this time taking a different road. I wasn't paying much attention to where I was going – my thoughts were still tying themselves up in knots.

After a while, though, I made myself concentrate on my surroundings. I was walking past a terrace of low, brick-built houses that fronted directly on to the street. All the houses were blotched with white, dusty patches – the builder must have put too much lime in the bricks.

At the end of the terrace was a chapel. This was also made of brick, but it was a deeper, more ruddy colour than the houses. The chapel was set back from the road. A strip of tarmac led through rows of gravestones to a set of double doors. One of these doors was open. Lights were on inside. A service was in progress.

Without thinking twice – hardly thinking once, really – I walked up the path and in through the door. Once inside, I saw that the chapel was more crowded than I'd expected. A few people turned round to see who this late arrival was, although not many. Most of them were staring at a small stage at the far end.

Mounted on the back wall was a portrait of the Saviour. On one side of it were the words 'Give Out Light' written in large gold letters, on the other side, 'Give Out Love'. In front of 'Give Out Light' was a frosted white bulb mounted on top of a barley-twist pole.

A woman was standing on the stage. Her grey hair was cut into a bob and she wore a long powder-blue dress. I found myself a seat near the back and close to the wall. There was a small shelf beside me with a decanter of water and two glasses on it.

Only as I sat down did I become aware that at least one person – and possibly more – was crying. Sobbing quietly to themselves. I should have left there and then, of course.

The trouble was I would have risked making a spectacle of myself, and so I stayed put.

The woman in blue stood perfectly still. In front of her was a small lectern. One of her arms was held in front of her, bent at the elbow. She had the back of her hand turned towards her, as if she was reading the time. Draped over her wrist was what appeared to be a necklace, or a length of chain.

She was studying this intently.

'Ronald,' she said after a while. 'Does anyone know a Ronald?'

There was silence, but a hopeful sort of silence, as if everybody was waiting for someone to fill it. The silence was broken by a dog barking – someone in the congregation must have brought one in. Then a man sitting two rows in front of me stuck his hand up.

'My father was called Donald,' he said.

'I didn't say Donald,' said the woman sternly. 'I said Ronald.'

The man lowered his hand.

'Ronald?' she said again, looking round. Still there were no takers. The woman didn't appear to be in the least bothered. 'I'll try again,' she said, and fell to further contemplation of the chain.

Several more minutes went by. 'Eric,' she said at last.

A few more hands went up now.

'Eric is a lovely-looking boy,' the woman said. 'In his late teens, or early twenties, I should say.'

The hands remained in the air. White fingers straining upwards. 'Where are you from, Eric?' asked the woman, leaning her head on one side.

The answer was not long in coming. 'Eric says he is from Bucklesham.'

There were groans at this. All but two of the hands went down. 'Eric passed over in France,' said the woman, 'but he's left a father behind him. And a mother too? No, not a mother. Sorry. She's already with him. What's the name of your father, Eric?' Again her head dipped down on one side. 'Eric says that his father's name is Doug.'

I heard a gasp. One of the two hands went down. The other stayed up for a few moments longer. Then this too was lowered. It belonged to a man who was sitting by himself near the front. Although it wasn't in the least cold in the church – it was quite close, in fact – he wore an overcoat. He also had a muffler wound round his neck.

'It's you, dear, isn't it?' said the woman in blue.

The man nodded. Then he said something I couldn't hear. The woman came down a set of steps from the stage and addressed him directly. 'Eric is fine, you know. They both are. Eric and Mum. Eric says he loves you very much and that you mustn't worry about either of them.'

'I hope I will be able to join them soon,' said the man in a matter-of-fact voice.

'You'll go when you're good and ready, dear,' said the woman. 'And not before. The last thing they want is for anyone to go over before their time. Is that clear?'

Again the man nodded. 'Is there anything else you can tell me?'

'Let me see . . . Eric is such a handsome boy. I can see he has your eyes. Such an honest face too. But he's got a scar on one of his hands. All the way up his arm. Is that from the war?'

'No. It's from when he was a boy. He fell on to some broken glass.'

'Yes, I thought it didn't look recent. You know what your

Eric is saying to me? He's saying, "I wish he'd laugh more."
Because you used to laugh a lot, didn't you?'

The man made no reply to this.

'See if you can do what Eric says, dear. Try to laugh a bit
more. Because it's not all doom and gloom out there, you
know. Now then, shall we see who else is trying to get
through?'

Next she got a Bernard, swiftly followed by an Eileen.
'I feel a lot of fluid here,' said the woman clutching her
stomach. 'Was that her problem? Tummy troubles?'

So it went on with this chorus of weeping rising and
falling, along with occasional interruptions from the dog.
'Can anyone take a Brian for me? A tall gentleman.
Something in his buttonhole. I think it's a carnation. They
won't come if someone won't accept them, you know.'

A woman's hand duly went up.

'You, dear? I asked Brian if he had a message and he said
no. He doesn't have anything particular to say. He just
wanted to say hello.'

'Yes,' said the woman. 'He never was a talkative one.'

By now I felt that I had no business here, sitting in on
other people's grief. I got to my feet, intending to slip out
through the still-open door. But I'd only taken a couple of
steps when I became aware that something had changed. It
must have been the quality of the silence.

I looked up. The woman in blue was again descending
from the stage. Now she was walking down the aisle in a
purposeful sort of way. She had a somewhat rolling gait.
I watched her come closer, not sure what to do.

When she reached me, she touched my shoulder. 'Are
you familiar with an Emily?' she asked.

'No,' I said, relieved. 'I don't believe I am.'

'A friend of your mother's? Possibly your grandmother's? A woman of about fifty years of age? Very light on her feet and a nice sense of humour?'

For the sake of being polite, I pretended to think about it. However, the moment couldn't be put off for long. 'It means nothing, I'm afraid.'

'Oh.'

She tapped her fingertips against her cheek as if she was ticking herself off. 'I see green fields. Yes . . . green fields which you left for a more important position. Now does that make any sense?'

Everyone had turned to face me. They had twisted round on their chairs, their faces large and curious.

'Possibly,' I said.

'And sand. Sand and green fields. Tell me, is somebody holding you up in your business?'

I didn't say anything.

'Yes,' she said. 'I thought so.'

She touched me again. This time her eyelids fluttered as if her eyes had rolled back in her head. When she next spoke she did so with absolute conviction. 'My message to you is plain: you must assert yourself. Do you understand me?'

Again I nodded.

'Good. Don't let anyone hold you back in your endeavours. Sometimes you just have to carry on regardless.'

She turned and walked back to the lectern. After that a man came on and said that he wanted to speak for all of us in thanking Miss Florence Thompson for a remarkable example of mediumship. He was sure this had brought a great deal of comfort to everyone.

A murmur of agreement ran through the congregation.

Once it had died away, he asked us to stand up and turn to Hymn 308 in our hymnals. From one side of the stage came the sounds of an organ. Very slow and dirge-like, as if whoever was playing it had their hands stuck in treacle. Above a low curtain a pile of blonde hair – presumably belonging to the organist – could be seen swaying from side to side.

First she ran through one verse to reacquaint us with the tune. And then in we all came:

> 'Lead, kindly Light, amid the encircling gloom,
> Lead Thou me on;
> The night is dark, and I am far from home;
> Lead Thou me on . . .'

I don't know how long it took me to walk back to Sutton Hoo House. A lot less time than it took me to walk into Woodbridge, that's for sure. As I turned into the driveway, my watch was showing just after seven thirty. Apart from a few dabs of cloud, the sky was still bright. With a bit of luck, I reckoned there should be another hour and a half of daylight left. Mrs Pretty's car was parked outside the back door. She must have come back from wherever she'd been to while I was in Woodbridge.

At the mounds, everything was just as we'd left it. That was a relief. I lit a pipe and climbed down the ladder. After I'd reached the bottom I took the ladder away from the side of the trench and laid it flat on the ground. I'm not sure why – it wasn't as if there was much chance of anyone else coming along. Even so, I wanted to make sure I was left alone.

When I unrolled the tarpaulins, the square of discoloured

earth showed up just as clearly as it had done before. I knelt down and set to, scraping and brushing. I didn't have to wait long. Two feet away from where I had found the coin, I came across a greenish band. It looked like the remains of a piece of copper. And then came another green band. Duller than the first – even after I'd brushed it down – but about the same width and length as before. Bronze hoops, I thought. That's what these will be. Bronze hoops from a barrel.

The light was starting to go now. When I looked at my watch it was already past nine o'clock. I couldn't believe it. I calculated how much time I'd waste going back and fetching a torch, and then decided that I'd just have to make do.

Sweat ran down my face, dripping on to the ground. I can't say how much later it was when I came across the piece of wood. To begin with, I assumed this must be the barrel. Or the remains of it at any rate. However, the wood was both larger and flatter than I would have expected. But if it wasn't a barrel, then what was it? There was another possibility, of course – it could be one of the collapsed roof timbers from the burial chamber.

I kept on brushing for a while. And then I decided to stop, just for a moment, before I went on. As soon as I'd put the brush down, I saw it. There was a small hole in the top left-hand corner of the piece of wood – hardly larger than the coin I had found earlier. While I was staring at it, wondering what to do next, I became aware of a presence nearby. A movement in the corner of my eye.

To begin with, I tried to ignore it – I didn't much care who it was, or what. And then came a whispered voice: 'Mr Brown.'

I looked up. Robert was crouched on one of the terraces. He had slippers on and was wearing his dressing gown.

'What are you doing here?'

'I saw the glow of your pipe. What have you found?'

'Nothing.'

'Can I come and have a look?'

'No, you can't.'

'Please, Mr Brown.'

'Not now, boy!' I said, much more loudly than I meant to. 'Can't you see I'm busy? Just go back to bed and leave me be.'

Aware that I'd spoken harshly, but too intent on what I was doing to make amends, I carried on as before. By the time I looked up again, Robert had gone. The light was fast disappearing now, the last few glimmers fading away. Maybe if there'd been more time, I wouldn't have done what I did next. I don't know. Probably that's just an excuse. The truth is I couldn't stop myself. At the same time, I was hardly even aware of what I was doing.

I pushed my finger into the hole. As I did so, I had the strangest feeling – it felt as if it was passing from one element to another. After a few minutes – I've no idea how long – I withdrew my finger. Then came the great wash of sadness, knocking me back.

Walking to the house, the sweat was cold against my skin. Above the rooftop the moon was so pale it was almost white. I rang the bell. Grateley stood in the doorway with the light bouncing off the walls behind him.

'Do you know what time it is, Basil?'

'Even so, I need to see her.'

He paused to consider this. Then he gave me a look. 'I'm sorry. But you'll just have to wait until morning.'

*

The next morning I did something I hadn't done in weeks –
I overslept. By the time I woke up it had gone six and it was
close to half past by the time I started work. I spent the
next two hours working my way round the piece of wood.
It was slow going as the wood kept flaking. Even so, it was
absorbing enough to stop me from thinking about anything
else.

At a quarter to nine I rang the bell, assuming that Mrs
Pretty would be up. Once again Grateley answered the
door. Once again he told me that Mrs Pretty was not
available. I asked if she was feeling poorly again. No, he
said. Not as far as he knew.

I couldn't understand what was going on – it didn't seem
to make any sense. Still, there was nothing to be done,
nothing I could think of anyway. So I went back and
carried on as before. At eleven o'clock Grateley appeared at
the mouth of the trench. He didn't make any comment on
the fact I was working. He just announced that Mrs Pretty
would see me now. We walked in silence back to the house.

As we were standing in the corridor, he said quietly,
'Hands, Basil.'

'What about them?'

'They could use a scrub.'

After I'd washed in the pantry, he led me through into
the hallway. The door to the sitting room was shut. I could
hear voices inside. The moment Grateley knocked, the
voices stopped.

The first person I saw was Charles Phillips – the man in
the bow tie. He was standing by the fireplace with one
elbow resting on the mantelpiece. I looked around.
Maynard and Reid Moir were behind the sofa. Although
Reid Moir stood perfectly still, something about the way he

was holding himself suggested he was writhing about inside.

Mrs Pretty was in the middle of the floor. 'Thank you so much for coming, Mr Brown,' she said. 'You know Mr Reid Moir and Mr Maynard, of course. Have you met Charles Phillips before?'

'In a manner of speaking,' I said.

'Now that we are all here, would everyone care to sit down?'

While there was a murmur of agreement at this, no one made any move to do so.

'Would you care to sit, Mr Brown?' Mrs Pretty asked.

'I'm fine where I am. Thank you very much, Mrs Pretty.'

No one spoke for a few moments. Then Mrs Pretty said, 'I have asked you here to discuss a rather delicate matter, Mr Brown.'

Already I'd decided to make a clean breast of it – there seemed no point doing anything else. Without further ado, I said, 'I know that Mr Phillips told me to stop digging. And I know that I had no business going back and carrying on last night –'

Before I could say anything else, Mrs Pretty held up her hand. 'I have no intention of rebuking you for your enthusiasm, Mr Brown. Quite the contrary. In fact, I want to make it plain from the outset that no one here has anything but the highest praise for the way you have conducted the excavation.'

Reid Moir nodded. So too, I saw, did Charles Phillips. It was at this point that I began to grow alarmed.

'None the less,' she went on, 'we must, all of us, take into account that this is a far bigger project than we could ever have imagined.'

Mrs Pretty paused, apparently to catch her breath. But before she could do so, Phillips stepped in. 'You mustn't take this personally, Brown,' he said.

'Take what personally, Mr Phillips?'

'Mmm? What I am about to say. First of all, I would like to second Mrs Pretty's opinion of your abilities. You have done a first-rate job here. Your knowledge of Suffolk soil is second to none. Frankly, I doubt if anyone could have done any better. However, as Mrs Pretty has already pointed out, this is now a very important dig, among the most important ever undertaken in this country. One that simply cannot be left in the hands of a somewhat ad hoc team from what, with the best will in the world, can only be described as a small provincial museum. Especially at this critical juncture. Therefore, with the full agreement of Mrs Pretty and, of course, with Mr Reid Moir and Mr Maynard's consent, I have assumed full control of the excavation. I will be working with a number of people from the British Museum. All of them top people in their fields. We in turn will be liaising closely with the Ministry of Works.'

Even then his words took a few moments to sink in.

'You're replacing me?' I said.

'That is not how I would choose to put it, Brown. I very much hope that you will feel able to carry on. Albeit in a more subordinate role.'

I looked across at Reid Moir. He gazed back at me. I've seen livelier-looking stares on a fishmonger's slab. Then I looked at Mrs Pretty. She was staring at the floor.

'When exactly are you taking over, Mr Phillips?' I asked.

'Immediately. From today.'

There was still a kind of swirl inside my head. Spinning everything round and round and then tossing it away.

'I see . . .' I said. 'In which case, I'd like to assure you that I'll do anything I can to help. In – in whatever way you see fit.'

Phillips turned to the others.

'You see? I told you that I did not anticipate any difficulties. None the less, I am grateful for your attitude, Brown. Very grateful.'

'Was there anything else?' I asked.

'No,' he said. 'No, I don't think so, unless . . .'

He glanced across at Mrs Pretty, but she didn't react. 'No, I think we have said everything that needed to be said.'

Grateley was waiting outside the door to lead me away. As we were passing the kitchen, Robert ran out. He stopped when he saw me. I started towards him, intending to give him a pat on the head. That was all. But as I did so, he flinched and ran back through the door.

Peggy Piggott
July 1939

After breakfast Stuart went for his morning walk. I sat in
the lounge and read the newspaper. Several of the other
guests were also there, sitting half-buried in their tatty
chairs, staring out with veiled, incurious eyes. They barely
moved even when the maid came in with the carpet
sweeper. Part of me wanted to pull them to their feet, the
women as well as the men, and spin them round, twirl them
out of themselves. This thought, though, was immediately
succeeded by a sense of guilt. What a troublesome nature
I have and how hastily I rush to judge people.

Some judgements, however, cannot be avoided. The
matter of the hotel, for instance. When Stuart was a child
he had come here on holiday with his parents. Ever since,
he had dreamed of coming back. But the place is not what
it was. That much was obvious on our first night as we sat
in the dining room, struggling to read grease-speckled
menus by the light of a flickering chandelier.

'I'm afraid they have rather let the place go, darling,' he
said. 'You don't mind, do you?'

'Of course not.'

Soon afterwards, in an attempt to drive the silence away,

a woman began to play the harp. She sat in the corner, plucking away at the strings with thick, inexpressive fingers. We both ordered the pork for our main course. The meat was so tough I had to use my knife like a saw. As we were chewing away, we caught one another's eye and started laughing. We both buried our faces in our napkins until our convulsions had passed.

Now I looked up to see that a boy had come into the lounge. He was wearing a brown uniform and swinging a silver dish.

'Piggott,' he called out.

A rustle of disapproval passed through the other guests. They did not care to be disturbed by any noise apart from the dinner gong.

'Piggott!' called out the boy again.

The ridiculous thing is I didn't recognize my own name. Not at first. The boy was about to go out again when I lifted my hand and said, 'Here.'

'Mrs Piggott?' he said, as if he couldn't quite believe it either.

'Yes.'

He held out the dish. It was much clouded by fingerprints. A brown envelope was lying there.

'Telegram for you.'

The words 'S. Piggott Esq.' were typed on the envelope. I picked it up, wondering who could have died or suffered some terrible accident. Telegrams always meant bad news; everybody knew that. Meanwhile, the other guests were staring at me from the depths of their chairs. All plainly suspecting me of being an impostor, yet willing me to open the envelope just the same.

I sat and waited for Stuart to come back, forcing myself

to concentrate on the newspaper. But I could only manage it for a few more minutes before I jumped to my feet and ran from the room – doubtless provoking another rustle of disapproval.

Outside it was raining. I stood beneath the awning and tried to see if I could catch sight of him. Rows of little Regency houses stretched in either direction, all painted in shades of cream, all with wrought-iron balconies facing towards the sea. Cliffs the colour of ox blood towered behind them. A few pedestrians were walking along the front, their heads down, their shoulders hunched.

Stuart, however, was not among them. I kept turning in one direction and then the other, all the time feeling a tide of panic rising inside me. At last I saw him. His mackintosh was stained with rain and his hair plastered over the dome of his head. He was only a few yards away when he looked up.

'Hello, darling! What are you doing out here?'

I didn't say anything; I just handed him the telegram. He didn't open the envelope until he had first taken off his coat, shaken it out and then hung it in the lobby. As he was reading, he pushed his bottom lip forward. Water ran down his face and collected there.

Then he began to laugh.

'What is it?'

He gave the telegram to me.

MAJOR FIND IN SUFFOLK STOP SHIP-BURIAL EVEN
BIGGER THAN OSEBERG STOP COME AT ONCE STOP
BRING WIFE STOP REGARDS PHILLIPS STOP

'I suppose I had better wire him back,' said Stuart.

'What are you going to tell him?'

'Why, that it's impossible, of course. Typical Phillips, issuing lordly commands and expecting everyone immediately to drop whatever they're doing.'

The panic must have churned me up. I was so relieved nothing was wrong that I didn't want the moment to pass.

'Are you sure you don't want to go?' I asked.

'Darling . . . we're on our honeymoon. There can be no question of our going. You're not seriously suggesting that we should, are you?'

'No, no . . . I mean, not unless you want to.'

'Of course not. Besides, it's not a matter of what I want . . . Strange, though, that Phillips should ask specially for you. Strange for him, that is. I suppose he must have read your paper on Bosnian lake villages. I did send it to him, and it is awfully good, of course. Do you think this ship can really be longer than the one at Oseberg – that was more than seventy feet, as I recall . . . For heaven's sake, what am I thinking of? Look, why don't you wait in the lounge, darling, and I'll go straight to the post office and wire him back.'

But before he could go, I put my hand on his sleeve. 'What if this find really is as exciting as Phillips says?'

'Yes, but even so . . .'

'This might be our last chance to be involved in something really significant for a long time. We might kick ourselves in years to come, when we're old.'

'Darling, no. It's simply not fair on you. Besides, the weather is bound to buck up soon. I only wish the hotel wasn't so *en ruine*.'

My fingers were still resting on his sleeve, the nails cut in unattractive little scallops. Staring at them, I said, 'Why don't you wire Phillips to tell him that we're coming?'

Stuart didn't reply, not immediately. When he did so, his

words all came out in a tumble. 'Are you quite sure? I mean, absolutely positive? Remember, you've never met Phillips. He can be a bit of a terror, you know. And there's bound to be trouble here. I booked us in for a full week.'

'Just leave that to me,' I said.

'Really? I just hate to think of you being disappointed, that's all.'

I stood on tiptoe and kissed him. 'You know you don't have to worry about that.'

The woman behind the reception desk seemed more upset than dismayed when I told her we were leaving. 'But you're in the bridal suite,' she kept repeating. In the end, she agreed that we would pay for the three nights we had spent there – this without my having to mention the pork, or the upholstery, or the wardrobe door that unaccountably swung open in the middle of the night.

After Stuart had paid the bill, the same boy who had brought the telegram took our cases out to the car and helped strap them on the back. Despite the car's being left out in the rain, the engine caught immediately. No doubt following instructions, the boy stayed outside and wanly waved us off.

At the end of the promenade, the road turned inwards, climbing all the time. Through the passenger window, I could see the horseshoe bay with its terraces of cream houses and the ox-blood cliffs that seemed to be pushing them towards the sea. As the road switched back and forth between the folds of hills, I couldn't entirely suppress a sense of relief. It felt as if we were climbing out of a hole.

That night we stayed with Stuart's sister and her husband in London – they live just around the corner from the rooms in Gower Street that I rented when I was studying for my diploma. The next morning we were on the road by nine o'clock. For the first time in days, the sun came out. Fortunately we had the road almost to ourselves and made good progress as far as Colchester.

On the other side of the town we pulled into a field to eat the sandwiches Stuart's sister had made. Several other cars were already parked there. People sat on the verge, eating and drinking. The men were in their shirtsleeves. A couple of the women, I saw, had rolled their stockings down to their ankles. Children were playing, throwing stones at a cattle trough. Whenever one of the stones hit, there was a loud booming sound. Every so often, one of the adults turned round and told them to stop, but they didn't take any notice.

We sat in the car with both the doors and windows open. 'You've never been to Suffolk, have you, darling?' Stuart asked.

'You make it sound like another country,' I said with my mouth full of sandwich.

'Oh, they're a funny lot, you know. Quite primitive, but proud of it. They rather see themselves as a race apart.'

'In what way?'

'An attitude really. A kind of bloody-mindedness and general dislike of authority. They like to think that they're out on the edge of things, while everyone else is either soft or ignorant.'

An hour later we crossed the border from Essex into Suffolk. After Stuart's description, I had half expected to see people jumping about in animal skins. However, all that happened was that the land grew flatter and flatter. The fields stretched away into the distance, broken only by lines of trees. It looked just like a prairie. Everything felt too big, too open, too exposed. Between the rows of barley and rye, the soil was the colour of canvas.

Wind, warm yet quite odourless, blew through the car. Even the cattle looked unsure of themselves, lost amid all this emptiness. What few houses we saw all seemed to have crudely built wooden porches and windows scarcely big enough to fit a person's head through. There also seemed to be an abnormal number of abandoned agricultural vehicles by the side of the road, most of them covered in parasols of cow parsley. Arcs of sand lay across the road and crunched beneath our wheels. Occasionally, I caught glimpses of the sea, although the flatness of the land made it almost impossible to tell where the land ended and the water began. Only a dull, metallic gleam gave it away.

It was after five o'clock by the time we arrived in Woodbridge. Stuart had arranged to meet Charles Phillips at the Bull Hotel. The Bull turned out to be a black and white coaching inn at the top of the town with a plaque on the front proclaiming that King Victor Emmanuel of Piedmont and Saxony had stayed on several occasions, but giving no indication as to what had brought him there.

A girl showed Stuart and me up to the room Phillips had reserved for us. The smell of beer, sour but strangely exotic, drifted up from the bar. Our room had twin beds and overlooked the square, with a shared bathroom at the end of the corridor. Stuart sat on one of the beds and pronounced it to be a definite improvement on Sidmouth. Then he came over to the window where I was standing and put his arm around my shoulder.

'Well done, darling,' he said.

'Well done for what?'

'I don't know. I hadn't thought that far.'

'You can't just say "well done" for no reason,' I said.

'Yes, I can. I can say whatever I want. Although, strictly speaking, I'm the one who deserves the congratulations.'

'For what exactly?'

'For persuading you to marry me, of course.'

I turned towards him and placed my hands flat against his chest. 'I don't know if I took that much persuading. Besides, impressionable girls are always falling in love with their professors. It must be one of the hazards of the job.'

'Not a hazard – not for me. Entirely a blessing . . . Now then,' he said, 'shall we go downstairs and see if Phillips is here?'

In fact, Phillips had not arrived, although he did so a few minutes later. While we had talked about Phillips on the journey up, nothing had quite prepared me for my first sight of him. He was a much larger man than I had expected. However, he carried his bulk, if not proudly, then with a considerable air of entitlement. By contrast, his bow tie was rather small, making him look like an inexpertly wrapped parcel.

When Stuart introduced me, his gaze ran up and down me in a quite blatant manner. Not just once either, but several times. Before sitting down, he glanced suspiciously at the other customers and then said, 'I think we should be safe here.'

Once seated, he beckoned the barman over. 'A pint of your best bitter for me,' said Phillips. 'I'm sure you'll join me, Stuart. And what would you like, my dear?' he asked.

'A half of best bitter, please.'

He looked at me again, as if to make sure he had heard correctly.

'And a half of best bitter,' he said.

When the beer arrived, Phillips drank half his in a single gulp. 'Right then, to business.' The ship, he said, was more than eighty feet long so far, with the likelihood that it would be close to a hundred feet by the time both ends had been exposed. 'As for dates, my estimate at this stage is anything from AD 600 to 800. I don't think we will be able to pinpoint it more accurately until we see what is in the burial chamber.

'Everything's been a bit of a mess so far. A local man called Brown was having a go under the auspices of Ipswich Museum. Self-taught, I'm afraid, and with everything that entails. He was on the verge of going right into the chamber, but fortunately I managed to step in before any real damage could be done. I'm hoping we will be joined by Frank Grimes from the Ordnance Survey. Possibly by Crawford too, if he can get away. Also, John Ward-Perkins is going to try to come from Rome. For the moment, however, it's just going to be the three of us.

'Now, I should tell you that the landowner, a Mrs Pretty, is a rather difficult lady, with some very fixed ideas of her own. There was even a bit of bother from the Ministry of Works, who had some lunatic scheme to erect a roof over the whole site. However, thanks to some nimble footwork on my part, I don't anticipate any further difficulties.'

'What's the situation with Ipswich, CW?' Stuart asked.

At this Phillips began to laugh. 'They're not very happy, I can tell you.'

'I bet they're not,' said Stuart, who had also started laughing.

'I thought Reid Moir might have a seizure when I told him I was taking over. What made it even worse is that he was still smarting over the reviews of his new book.'

'What's this one about?' Stuart asked.

'Flints!' exclaimed Phillips. 'Paralysingly dull, by all accounts. Do you know, I don't think he's forgiven me over that whole business with the aerial photographs.'

'You must tell Peggy what happened, CW.'

'Shall I? It was the most amusing thing.'

Phillips looked at me expectantly.

'Do, please,' I said.

'Very well. Reid Moir was awfully excited about what he claimed – insisted, would be nearer the mark – was evidence of a sunken village off the coast near Walberswick. He showed me the photographs and asked what I thought of his extraordinary find, plainly expecting me to salute him for his brilliance. I looked at them and said, my dear man, have you never seen oyster beds before?'

At this, they both began to laugh again, even more loudly than before. When the laughter had died away, Phillips held up his glass and called for more drinks.

'And how about events in the wider world?' Stuart asked. 'How do you think they might affect us?'

Phillips looked at him blankly. 'The wider world?'

'The Germans, CW . . .'

'Germans . . .' said Phillips in surprise. 'I don't recall a ship-burial ever being discovered in Germany.'

'No, no. I meant, the possibility – likelihood, even – of war.'

'Oh,' said Phillips. 'That. Well, there's no doubt that we will have to get our skates on. The BM has already started packing up its more fragile pieces and putting them in a tube tunnel beneath the Aldwych. I'd say we have three weeks at most to complete the excavation.'

It wasn't until that moment that I realized how

successfully I had used the excitement of our marriage to distract myself from the imminence of war. But the fact that I was having this realization at all probably meant the distraction had started to wear off.

Soon afterwards, Stuart excused himself. 'Beer,' he explained with an apologetic wince. 'It runs straight through me.'

Left alone with Charles Phillips, I struggled to think of something else to say. It was not easy, especially as he made no effort to instigate conversation. Instead, he sat polishing his spectacles with his handkerchief. This made me even more tongue-tied than usual. After a lengthy period of silence, I grew a little desperate.

'Are you also staying in the Bull, Mr Phillips?' I asked.

'Unfortunately, yes,' he said. 'I had been expecting to stay at Sutton Hoo House. That would have been far more convenient. Unfortunately, there appears to have been some sort of misunderstanding with Mrs Pretty – the lady I mentioned earlier.'

Once again he lapsed into silence. Once again I strained for something to say.

'I wanted to tell you how flattered I was that you specifically asked for me to come here.'

Phillips glanced up at this, but did not reply.

'I know Stuart sent you my paper on Bosnian lake villages,' I went on. 'It was awfully good of you to read it.'

He looked at me for longer than before, then said, 'Very stimulating.'

'That means a great deal. I only hope I will be able to repay your faith in me.'

'I have no doubt you will.'

'It's just that I haven't done that much actual fieldwork.'

129

He shook his head impatiently. 'Never mind about that.'

'I wouldn't want you to think I was more experienced than I actually am.'

'You have all the key attributes,' he said. 'That's all that matters.'

'I do? I'm sure I'm being frightfully slow, Mr Phillips, but I don't follow you.'

'It's perfectly simple. Look at me. Now, what do you see?'

'A man,' I said uncertainly.

'Yes, obviously a man. But a man of a certain size. I happen to have large bones; it runs in my family. Stuart has smaller bones than me, although even he must be around the twelve-stone mark. You, however, by virtue of your sex, are a good deal smaller and lighter than either of us. The ship is in a very delicate condition. You might say it scarcely exists at all, except for the rivets. Everything else is just hard sand. Put too much weight on it and the whole thing could disintegrate. It therefore seems sensible that I should supervise matters from outside the trench, while you will be able to get on with the actual digging. There,' he said, 'is that clear enough?'

'Am I – am I to understand that you only asked me here because of my size, Mr Phillips?'

Behind his spectacles, his eyes were quite small and bright. 'Exactly,' he said.

The next morning we drove out to the dig. It was only a couple of miles away, on the other side of the estuary to Woodbridge. The driveway passed through a tunnel of beech trees. Sunlight flickered between the leaves, casting patterns on the gravel below. The house itself was a large white Edwardian building, set up on a bluff above the river, complete with squash court and garages.

Despite my having tried to envisage the site beforehand, I was still astonished by what I saw. There was a majesty about the sweep and scale of the ship that far exceeded any expectations. There was also something intensely moving about its tenacious hold on survival. About the way in which it had resisted obliteration by transforming itself from one substance into another. From wood into sand. It was like a giant apparition lying there before us. I looked at Stuart and saw that he was just as affected.

Three men were lined up on one side of the trench, apparently waiting for us. Phillips introduced them. 'Mr Spooner and Mr Jacobs, and this is Mr Brown, who did such sterling work on the earlier stages of the dig.'

Mr Brown was a small, ferrety-faced man wearing an ancient tweed jacket and what might once have been a matching tweed cap. After we had all shaken hands, Stuart and I began by dividing the centre of the ship into a grid. We then laid down a planning frame and marked off the squares with lengths of string. The men, meanwhile, were put to work shifting the spoil heaps – Phillips had decided these were too near the ship and should be moved further away. With only one wheelbarrow between them, this proved to be a lengthy business.

Stuart and I, however, made rapid progress. Once we had divided the ship into squares, we started cleaning down the south side of the burial area. During the morning Mrs Pretty and her son, Robert, came out to see how we were getting along. Once again, Phillips performed the introductions. Mrs Pretty seemed much too old to be the mother of such a young son. The boy, Robert, twisted shyly away while he was being introduced and then ran off towards the spoil heaps as soon as Phillips had finished.

That afternoon, Stuart started to make a proper map of the site, while I carried on as before. At seven o'clock we finished for the day and drove back to the Bull. As I was muddy from the dig, I decided to take advantage of the fact that the bathroom was free.

The water hiccuped and spat from the hot tap as the bathroom filled with steam. Standing on the cork mat, I tested the water with my foot. It was hotter than I had expected – so hot my toes instinctively clenched – although not too hot to tolerate. First I swung one leg in and then the other. The bath was wonderfully big; you could have fitted two people in it with no trouble at all.

As I lowered myself down, I could feel the line between hot and cold sliding up my body, from my calves up to my hips. Warming my blood by horizontal degrees. Once I was fully immersed, I lay back, gasping as the water closed over my chest, seeing the steam part with the force of my breath. I could feel the heat against my eyeballs, passing down my throat.

Enveloped in steam, shiny with soap, I spread my hands and let my arms float out on either side of me. As I did so, my thoughts also started to lighten and float. I found myself thinking about the flat in Great Ormond Street which I had moved into at the start of my second year at the university. Apart from the Georgian windows and a black marble fireplace, there was nothing particularly special about it. Pipes shrieked whenever the water was turned on, while strips of wallpaper fell from the walls like plane trees shedding their bark. The furnishings – Lloyd Loom chairs, pine table, mahogany tallboy – were a utilitarian jumble, while at night mice ran about beneath the floorboards.

Yet it was the first place where I had ever felt truly at home, able to be myself. From a second-hand shop in Theobalds Road, I bought an old EMG gramophone with a brass horn and a box of needles. For an extra five shillings, the man offered to sell me a case of records. Some of the records were hopelessly scratched, while others were missing their labels. A few, however, were in a perfectly playable condition. One was Max Bruch's First Violin Concerto.

I had never heard it before, but from the moment it began I was filled with a kind of ecstatic familiarity. The music seemed to reach down deep inside me, touching me and transforming me. Dressed only in my underclothes, I began to dance around the flat. Not knowing what I was doing, but making my own steps. Improvising as best as I could. Flinging out my legs and throwing back my head. Catching glimpses of my reflection in the long mirror as I spun past. My body no longer lumpish and ungainly, but sleek and graceful. Soaring and then tumbling in this rhapsodic state of bliss.

Lying now in the bath, I started to sway gently in time to the music in my head. At first, the water threatened to slop over the sides, but as it balanced on the lip of the bath it grew suddenly viscous and slid back down the porcelain. Cupping my hands, I lifted them up and let the water trickle down over my head and shoulders.

As I was doing so, the bathroom door opened.

Immediately, I covered myself up as best I could. Through the steam I could see a face – a man's face. Then a muffled voice said, 'I'm frightfully sorry.' The door closed.

It took me a few moments to realize that the man had been Stuart. Stepping out of the bath, I quickly towelled myself dry.

When I returned to the bedroom, Stuart was sitting in the armchair with a book open in his lap. He didn't say anything when I came in. It was while I was brushing my hair that he said quietly, 'I could have been anyone, you know.'

'I'm sorry.'

'You forgot to lock the door.'

'I know . . . I didn't think.'

'Of course, it doesn't matter – seeing how it was me. But it might not have been me. That's the point. You will be more careful in future, won't you, darling?'

'I promise you it won't happen again,' I said.

He smiled at me over the top of his spectacles, then returned to his book.

As we were on our way out of the hotel the next morning, the receptionist gave us a note from Charles Phillips. It said that he had gone to Cambridge and would not be back until some time in the afternoon.

Stuart and I started where we had left off. He carried on making a map of the site, while I continued trowelling and sieving in the southern corner of the burial chamber. The clouds soon parted and lifted. By the time Mrs Pretty and Robert came out, the sun was shining more fiercely than it had done all summer. I wished I had packed a hat – my skin turns an off-puttingly dark shade of brown in the sun.

At eleven o'clock, Mrs Pretty's butler brought out a tray with two jugs of lemon barley water on it and some glasses. We all broke off and drank our fill. No one said very much. I know that I am apt to misread people's moods, but it seemed to me to be an eager, expectant sort of silence. A sense of anticipation that everyone shared, but no one wished to acknowledge out loud.

When we had finished, I set to again. The crust of earth felt quite solid beneath my feet. Dust rose all round, caking my hands and stiffening my hair. Normally, there is something not simply absorbing about narrowing one's focus to such a small area, but also soothing. Your world has shrunk to a few square inches of earth and nothing else matters. Nothing else can be allowed to matter.

Now, though, I found that my concentration had been affected. I wanted to blame it on the sunlight, while knowing perfectly well that it wasn't the sunlight at all. My hands continued working away, but my mind did not feel connected to them. Instead, it kept wandering off on its own, always towards the same place. There was one image I couldn't dislodge, no matter how hard I tried. It had been swimming around in my mind all night, looming before me whenever I tried to convince myself that I was on the verge of sleep.

All the time I saw Stuart's face looking round the bathroom door. Except that now the steam had parted and I could see his expression quite clearly. Shocked, but not just shocked – something more than that. I told myself that I must be mistaken, that I was working myself into a state over nothing. Only this didn't work either. The more I told myself, the less convincing it became.

Stuart is such a fine man: wise, kind and even-tempered. I feel so very lucky – so blessed – to have found him. It is an added blessing that we have shared interests to bind us together. This, I am convinced, is the key to an enduring relationship.

Yet I know that I must be doing something wrong. That I must be disappointing Stuart in some critical way. I cannot tell if it is my troublesome nature, or my appearance, or both. I so want to make myself attractive to him that it's having quite the opposite effect. I am driving him away. But I have no idea how to make anything better, or who to turn to for advice.

As my hands kept on trowelling, my eyes started to mist over. Angrily, I wiped the moisture away. It was only then that I saw what was lying in front of me. My first thought was that I must have dropped something. Or that someone else must have done. It looked so bright, so raw. So absurdly new.

I reached out and my fingers touched a small, hard object. At the same time I heard myself saying, 'Oh,' in a faraway voice. Then I picked it up. Lying in the palm of my hand was a gold pyramid. It was flattened on top and decorated with what appeared to be tiny pieces of garnet and lapis lazuli. In the centre of the flattened top was a square made up of even tinier blue and white chequered glass.

'Stuart,' I said, my voice sounding faint and scarcely my own.

He was sitting on the bank, drawing. I saw him lift up his head.

'What is it, darling?'

'Will you come here?'

When I put the pyramid in Stuart's hand, I was struck by how much smaller it looked than it had done in mine. He stared at the pyramid for what felt like a long time before asking, 'Where did you find this?'

I didn't say anything; I just pointed down at the ground.

When I did so, his face broke into a smile. It was such a big smile that it seemed to wrap itself around his face.

'You clever girl,' he said. Then he stepped forward and hugged me. 'You clever, clever girl.'

I buried my forehead in his shoulder. I didn't want him to see that I had been crying. Besides, I could hardly recall what I'd been making such a fuss about.

Then, in a much louder voice, he said, 'May I have your attention, everyone? Peggy, my wife, has found something that I am sure will interest you.'

A quickening murmur ran round the site. Everyone strained forward, looking over the bank into the ship. We crossed to the ladder. I went up first. Mrs Pretty and her son were waiting at the top.

'What is it?' Robert was yelling. 'What have you found?'

'It appears to be a piece of jewellery,' I told him.

'Gold?'

'Oh, it's gold, all right,' said Stuart, coming up behind me. 'Gold with very intricate cloisonné work.'

Although I can't imagine this meant a great deal to Robert, it did nothing to dampen his enthusiasm. As I handed the pyramid to Mrs Pretty, he kept jumping up and down beside her.

'May I see, Mama? Please may I see?'

Rather than pass the pyramid to him, Mrs Pretty held it out between her thumb and forefinger. He put his face very close to it, scrunching up his forehead and squinting at it from as many angles as possible. Afterwards, she let the men have a look – they had also gathered round and were showing a lively interest.

'You found this, did you, Mrs Piggott?' Mrs Pretty asked.

'Yes,' I said. 'I believe so . . . I mean, yes, I did.'

137

At this, she grasped my hand, much more strongly and more warmly than I would have expected.

'Well done, my dear. Many congratulations. What a wonderful discovery.'

Part of me wanted to tell her that it had just been lying there. That all I had had to do was bend down and pick it up. But I said nothing. However ill-deserved all this praise may have been, I didn't want it to go away. Not completely. My mouth was very dry. I kept hoping Mrs Pretty's butler would reappear with more barley water, but he never did.

While we were standing around in a dazed sort of way, Mr Brown came over and asked if I wouldn't mind telling him where I had found the pyramid.

'I can easily show you, if you like,' I said. 'If you'd just come down the ladder.'

He glanced around before saying, 'I'd better not, thank you.'

'Don't worry. I'll hold on to the bottom.'

'No, no,' he said, and gave a laugh. 'It's not that. Mr Phillips has said he doesn't want me going anywhere near the burial chamber.'

'Mr Phillips? Why on earth would he say such a thing?'

'I don't exactly know, although I dare say he has his reasons. Perhaps you could show me from here.'

I pointed down into the ship. 'Just down there,' I told him. 'See that greenish band there? Just to the left of it.'

After gazing at the spot for some time, he nodded, thanked me again and walked away. In the end, it was Stuart who suggested in a slightly embarrassed fashion that we should all go back to work.

*

138

When Phillips came back during the afternoon, he promptly flew into a rage at not having been there when the discovery was made. When shown the pyramid by Stuart, he glared at it, as if both stupefied and affronted by its presence.

'Ye gods,' he muttered.

'Peggy found it, CW,' Stuart told him.

Phillips didn't react to this; he just kept on glaring at the pyramid. Soon afterwards the light turned an odd lemony colour and rain began to fall. At first, it looked as if it would be no more than a shower, but then came several claps of thunder. These were followed by an extraordinary sight. A dark curtain was being drawn down the centre of the estuary, wet on one side, dry on the other. It might have been moving on rails, brushing against the surface of the water.

We all helped to put the covers back on and then took shelter beneath the trees. The rain grew heavier, clattering on the leaves and sending brown rivulets running down the spoil heaps. In the wood, Robert amused himself by jumping from one mossy hummock to another. By six it was plain that we were not going to be able to continue. Phillips told the men they could go, as soon as they had made sure the tarpaulins were securely fastened.

We drove back to Woodbridge with Phillips following. I sat beside Stuart with the window open and the thundery breeze buffeting against my face. My limbs were so heavy I felt I had molasses flowing through my veins. As we drew up outside the Bull, the street lights were already being turned on due to the weather. Orange balls of light stood out against the dark grey sky.

'Oh, Lord,' said Stuart as he was putting the car keys into his pocket.

'What's the matter?'

He withdrew his hand and unfolded his fingers. Under the street lights, the gold pyramid gave off a soft oystery glow.

'I had been intending to give it to Mrs Pretty, but it must have completely slipped my mind. What do you think I should do, darling?'

'Don't do anything,' I said.

'But shouldn't I tell Phillips?'

'Not now – not tonight. Just remember to give it to Mrs Pretty in the morning.'

When we walked through the front door, I could hear the sound of laughter coming from the bar. Clouds of smoke billowed into the corridor. We waited for Phillips to come in. I had assumed he would march straight past the bar and head for his room. To my surprise, though, he rubbed his hands together and said, 'I think this calls for a celebration, don't you?'

'I should say so,' agreed Stuart.

The bar was crowded, with no spare seats. Even Phillips was unable to make much headway against the throng of drinkers. Stuart and I attempted to reach the bar by another route. But we hadn't gone far when our path was blocked by a small round man.

'I know who you are,' said the man, rocking confidently back and forth. 'I've seen you in here before.'

'Have you now?' said Stuart.

'You're one of those archaeologists working over at Sutton Hoo.'

'That's right.'

'How are you getting on then?'

'Oh, not too bad. Not too bad at all.'

'Found any gold, have you, old boy?'

Stuart leaned towards him. 'As a matter of fact,' he said in a confidential sort of manner, 'my pockets are full of it.'

The man laughed so hard at this that he might have overbalanced if it hadn't been for the press of people. 'Marvellous, marvellous. You must have a drink, then.'

'Thank you,' said Stuart. 'I think I could do with one.'

'Here,' said the man to the occupants of one of the nearby tables. 'Mind your manners, lads. There's a young lady here with nowhere to sit.'

The men stood up with no sign of resentment. Drinks were fetched and set before us. Before we drank, we all hoisted our glasses at our benefactor, who lifted his in return.

'Congratulations, darling,' said Stuart, with his glass still held aloft.

'Yes,' said Phillips. 'Cheers. People spend entire lifetimes waiting for a discovery like this. It hardly seems fair that it should happen to one so inexperienced. None the less, here's to you, my dear.'

The beer had such a delicious peaty taste that I was reluctant to swallow it. Instead, I kept swilling it around in my mouth until the taste had disappeared. Afterwards I took another mouthful and did the same thing.

'Now, let's think about period, shall we?' said Phillips, sitting forward with one hand planted on his knee.

'As you mentioned before, CW,' said Stuart, 'if the boat is roughly contemporaneous with Oseberg, then that would suggest anything between AD 600 and 800. My initial feeling was that we were looking at something nearer the latter end of the scale. However, the jewellery rather changes all that.'

141

'Yes, yes. Go on.'

'Well, the only comparative jewellery that I can think of is the piece that Kendrick found at Dorchester on Thames in the early twenties. He believed this to date from the early part of the seventh century. Kendrick, of course, was roundly ridiculed for making such a suggestion. The general feeling was that a piece of such intricate workmanship couldn't possibly be that old. In effect, Kendrick was invited to recant, although he refused to do so. I think we now have to consider the possibility that he might have been right, after all.'

'We may,' said Phillips. 'We may indeed have to consider that possibility. Let's also consider the coin that Brown found before I arrived. This morning, I took it to Cambridge for Kendrick himself to examine. As you know, East Anglia did not have a coin-based economy until the eighth century at the earliest. However, a number of Anglo-Saxon inhumations have been discovered with coins in them dating back to around AD 575. The coins are assumed to have been used for symbolic purposes – most probably for placing in the mouths of the dead in order to facilitate their passage from this world to the next.

'I think it's fair to say that Kendrick was considerably taken aback when I showed him our coin,' added Phillips with satisfaction. 'Frankly, he could hardly believe his eyes. It took me a while to convince him it wasn't a prank, something a student had knocked up in the lab.'

Stuart began to laugh. His eyes were sparkling. I don't think I had ever seen him look so happy.

'The first thing Kendrick said was that he was quite certain it wasn't from East Anglia at all. Although he was only able to give it a cursory examination, he believes it to be a *tremiss* from Merovingian Gaul, dating from between AD 575 and 625.'

Phillips took another drink and pressed his lips together. 'Considering all this, now what do we have? We have a buried Anglo-Saxon ship, almost 100 feet in length, with what appears to be a burial chamber at the heart of it. A burial chamber that would appear to be completely intact. I suppose we have to consider the possibility that both the coin and the gold pyramid were placed there at a later date, but I doubt if even Reid Moir would give that one serious credence. No, the inference must surely be that this is the grave of someone important, and that the jewellery is part of his grave goods.'

'But surely –' I broke in.

'Yes?'

I knew that I must not appear too excitable. That I must make sure my voice was properly measured.

'Well,' I said, 'if that is true, and if Professor Kendrick is right, then surely that would alter our entire understanding of the Dark Ages?'

There was a pause after I had finished and I began to wonder if I had said something foolish.

Then Phillips went, 'Mmm . . . it would rather.'

The curtains had been drawn in our bedroom and the beds turned down. Only the bedside light was switched on. Stuart stretched out his arms in front of him. 'It's been quite a day, hasn't it?'

'Quite a day.'

'You should feel very proud of yourself, darling.'

'Should I?'

'You know perfectly well you should.'

143

Just as he had done earlier, Stuart came towards me and wrapped his arms around my shoulders. His tweed jacket had a reassuring smell, of solidity and permanence. It was the sort of smell that could banish doubts and fears, possibly for ever. I turned my face up towards his, wanting above all to feel his mouth on mine, if only for a moment. It would have been the crowning of a perfect day.

Stuart, meanwhile, was looking over my shoulder towards the window, as if peering through the drawn curtains at the street outside. Without relaxing his grip, he tilted his head down towards mine. We stayed like that for some time. Then he gently extricated himself and went back over to the armchair.

The nonchalance with which Stuart undressed only made my self-consciousness all the more pronounced. He undid his boots, folded his trousers over the arm of the chair and buttoned up his pyjamas. When I got into bed, the sheets were cold against my skin. I had to push my feet down to the bottom of the bed in one movement for fear that they would become stuck halfway. Even then, there was a moment when I doubted if the warmth of my body would be enough to drive the cold away.

'Ready?' he said.

'Ready.'

'Right, then. Sleep well, darling.'

'And you.'

He reached over and turned off the light.

Instead of leaving the car by the squash court, as he had done before, Stuart continued along the track all the way to the mounds and parked beside the shepherd's hut. The men were already there with their shovels, awaiting instructions.

Everything proceeded as before: the procession from the house, the setting up of Mrs Pretty's chair, supplemented today by a golfing umbrella. Before we started, Stuart handed the pyramid to Mrs Pretty, apologizing for not having done so the day before.

I then continued in the same part of the chamber, while Stuart moved to the westernmost corner. Phillips patrolled up and down the edge of the trench, monitoring our progress. An hour or so after we started Stuart called me over. He had uncovered the rim of a large bronze bowl. Inside it, showing up as this circular protrusion in the sand, was what appeared to be the rim of a second, slightly smaller bowl. This second bowl had a definite collar-like formation on one side which might have been the remains of a lid. Rather than try to remove either of the bowls, Stuart decided to leave them there until the ground around had been lowered to the same level.

Soon afterwards came another object – the first of several iron clamps. On the same axis as the clamps was a large, apparently amorphous mass of decayed wood. Stuart believed – and Phillips agreed – that these clamps must have been used in the construction of the burial chamber and that the piece of wood was part of one of the walls, or possibly even the roof.

The sluggishness that I'd felt the day before had not gone away. Although I had slept, I had only managed to do so in a restless, fretful sort of way. In my dreams, the sky was black, with planes obliterating what was left of Sutton Hoo, and probably us as well. It seemed an especially cruel sort of joke that we should be unearthing the remains of one civilization just as our own appeared to be on the brink of annihilation. In the *Daily Telegraph* that morning, I

had read that the Germans were reported to be continuing
their build-up of forces in the port of Danzig. A Polish
frontier guard had been shot and killed – it was presumed
by SS officers stationed in the city. Meanwhile, a doodle
by Field Marshal Goering, the head of the German air
force, had been analysed by a handwriting expert. The
expert had concluded that the person who had drawn the
doodle was feeling 'very much in control and rather
unresponsive'.

Just before lunch, I came across a mass of folded and
stitched leather. It looked just like a pad of unburnt
newspaper from a bonfire. Although much decayed, several
of the stitches were still intact. Phillips suggested putting it
in some water. A bowl was brought and the mass of leather
immersed. Nothing happened for a while. Then, very
slowly at first, the leather began to unfurl.

As it did so, I realized this was the sole of a shoe or
sandal. I stared in fascination as it bent and stretched. It
looked exactly as if a living foot was still inside, taking on
substance before me. But when I took it out of the bowl, it
disintegrated immediately. All that was left was this
weightless slime that fell from my fingers in long brown
strands.

When we broke for lunch we all – the men included – sat
on the top of the trench, our legs stretched out in front of
us, eating the sandwiches that Mrs Pretty had provided. At
one point Phillips dropped an apple. It rolled down the
bank, bounced across two of the terraces and came to rest
in the middle of the burial chamber. Without being asked,
Robert slid down the bank and went to retrieve it for him. I
saw the appalled expression on Phillips's face as Robert
scampered across the crust of sand. However, he managed

to make a reasonably plausible job of thanking him for his trouble when his apple was returned.

But his mood deteriorated sharply when Mrs Pretty informed him that she had invited a number of local people to a sherry party on the following Tuesday so that they could have a chance to inspect the ship. She apologized for not telling him earlier, but said that it had slipped her mind in all the excitement. She also mentioned that her nephew was on a bicycling holiday in East Anglia and would be arriving that afternoon. A keen amateur photographer, he hoped to be able to take some pictures of the excavation.

I could see that both of these pieces of information were extremely unwelcome to Phillips. He could hardly say anything, though. Only the curtness of his replies gave away the scale of his displeasure.

Once we had finished eating, we set to again. Mrs Pretty disappeared back beneath her umbrella, trying without much success to keep Robert beside her. Above our heads tiny silver aeroplanes darted about among the clouds. The sun was even hotter now; the earth had been baked quite dry and in places was starting to turn powdery and run. Stuart, I knew, was concerned that the combination of wet and heat could cause fissures to open up all over the boat. But the only thing we could do was keep everything covered when we were not working.

The hissing noise I heard sounded like air escaping from a bicycle tyre. I looked up. Stuart was bent over, facing away from me. He didn't move. Just as I was wondering where the sound could have come from, I heard another hiss.

I went over. He had uncovered what appeared to be a layer of wood. The wood was plainly very rotten – it was practically transparent. The streaks of grain were held together by only the thinnest of skins.

'Can you see that?' he said quietly. His finger was extended. 'There, in the background.'

Standing up, I couldn't see what he meant. However, the moment I squatted down, I saw it straight away. Behind this screen of decayed wood, I made out a faint gleam. When I shifted my head fractionally to the side, the gleam vanished. But as soon as I moved my head back – by the same fractional amount – back it came again.

'You do see what I'm talking about, don't you, darling?' he asked.

I nodded.

'Thank God for that,' he said. 'I was beginning to think my eyes were playing tricks.'

Stuart kept brushing away. Every few seconds he broke off to check on his progress, rocking back on to his knees, then tilting forward again. As he did so, I could see more gold emerging from behind this powdery screen. There appeared to be three separate pieces. One looked identical to the pyramid I had found the day before. The other two were small gold plaques, both around two inches in length – one flat and triangular, the other with a more rounded end. Each had the same intricate threading of gold around an inlay of garnets.

All of them were so beautiful. So delicate and yet so pristine. They were like emissaries from another world, undimmed by the mass of centuries that had passed since they had been last seen. Or rather, it was as if all those centuries had counted for nothing. Time had simply flown by between then and now.

Neither of us could look away. Stuart extended one arm

towards me. I took hold of his wrist. 'I never imagined . . .' he said. 'I thought yesterday might have been a fluke. But this – my God. What are we going to do?'

There was a note of helplessness in his voice. Tightening my grip, I found myself saying, 'Don't worry, darling. It'll be all right.'

'Yes,' he said. 'Yes, of course it will . . . We'd better call the others. I suppose.'

But in the event, there was no need to. Something had already alerted Charles Phillips.

'What is it?' he was saying. 'What have you found?' He was quickly joined by Robert. The tone of their voices sounded identical, both equally excited.

'It's more gold, CW,' said Stuart. 'Quite a bit more gold, in fact.'

Phillips, I saw, was puce with frustration. He paced back and forth along the top of the trench, almost colliding with Robert as he did so. After he had done this a few times, he stopped and said, 'Just don't move, either of you. Is that perfectly clear? I am coming down the ladder.'

As quickly as he could, Phillips began to descend. At this point discipline rather broke down. He was followed by Mrs Pretty and then by Robert. Throughout this, the men – Mr Brown, Mr Spooner and Mr Jacobs – remained on the bank, looking down.

Meanwhile, in the trench, the five of us – Stuart and myself, Charles Phillips, Mrs Pretty and Robert – knelt and gazed at what had been found. Looking at the pieces of jewellery, I was overcome by an enormous sense of insignificance. Not just my own insignificance, but everybody's. I felt as if we were all insects who had been tipped on to our backs and were waving our legs vainly at the sky.

After a while Phillips ordered everyone from the chamber. Everyone apart from Stuart and myself. 'What would you like us to do, CW?' Stuart asked.

Behind his spectacles, Phillips's eyes were still swimming about. Slowly, they steadied and sharpened.

'Do?' he said. 'Carry on, of course.'

Once we had removed the two gold plaques and the gold pyramid, we continued in the same southern corner of the chamber. Stuart took one side of a square and I took the opposite one. Together, we worked our way towards the centre.

As on the previous day, but even more so now, I felt there was this enormous gap between my outward behaviour and my inner world. On the outside, I was perfectly controlled. I could see my fingers holding the pastry brush, sweeping carefully and methodically at the soil. My mind, though, was a riot. Dazzled one moment, then plunged into confusion the next.

But even in the midst of this headspin, I knew with absolute certainty that I would unearth something else. It never occurred to me for a moment that I wouldn't. All the time my hands worked unhesitatingly away, just as if they were being guided. They might have had strings attached to them. And when I did find something, I felt no sense of surprise at all. I felt only relief that I had done what I had been supposed to do.

I had uncovered a kidney-shaped object. This too was made of gold. It was approximately three inches in length with one straight edge. Three tiny rectangles protruded from the one straight edge. Each of these rectangles was the same distance apart.

Stuart appeared beside me as I was staring at it. 'What

do you think, darling?' he asked. His voice was more businesslike now; the helplessness had disappeared completely.

'Possibly a purse lid?' I suggested. 'These pieces here look as if they might be hinges.'

'They do, don't they? Shall we have it out?'

As soon as I had prised the purse lid free, I saw that it had been lying face-down. On the reverse side, it was decorated in a similar style to the pyramids, inlaid with garnets and pieces of millefiori glass. Once I had blown the remaining grains of sand away, I saw something else. There was a pattern there. Two birds had been etched into the gold. Their eyes had also been picked out with tiny garnets – smaller than pinheads. Both of the birds had their heads back and their claws extended.

At that moment, I wanted to go away. More than anything else, I wanted to be back at the Bull. Lying in my bed and holding on to the sides in case it should race away with me. I wasn't sure I could cope with any more. Not without falling into a swoon or disgracing myself in some way. However, it was not to be.

'Darling . . .' said Stuart. 'Look.'

I followed his gaze. Under where I had found the purse lid – beneath a faint covering of sand – were lying a number of coins. About twenty as far as I could tell. It only needed a few strokes of Stuart's brush to bring them back into the open. Some of the coins, I saw, had crosses on one side of them. Although discoloured with age, they appeared quite undamaged.

Sticking to a number of the coins were threads of fibre, presumably from the bag they had once been in. Without dislodging too many of the threads, we placed the coins on a plate, then passed them up to the top of the trench. Everyone stood ranged along the bank. They all seemed lit up with excitement.

When we had finished taking down the ground level by another two to three inches, Stuart moved to the square on his left. I just knelt and watched him working. Doing so, I had this strange sense that he too knew exactly what he was looking for. Almost as if he was coming back for something he had stowed earlier for safe-keeping.

The first thing I saw was what appeared to be gold worms, wriggling away. Then I realized this was a host of tiny, serpentine creatures, all entwined around one another. Next came three raised circles, like buttons. As Stuart continued brushing, whatever he was uncovering grew steadily bigger. At one end was a hole bisected by a single gold bar. At the foot of the gold bar was a fourth circle. Although this circle was not domed, it was engraved with the same writhing serpentine creatures as before.

He kept going, working with the most minute movements. Somehow it felt appropriate that an object of such exquisite construction should be excavated by someone with such precision, such delicacy.

'There,' he said. 'I think that's about it.'

Now I could see instantly what he had found. It was a belt buckle. But larger and more ornate than any belt buckle I had ever seen before. It must have been close to six inches long and half that in width. Everything was made out of gold. The horizontal bar formed part of the clasp, while the domed studs must have originally fastened it to the belt.

Without speaking – without needing to – the two of us lifted it up with our fingertips. The imprint of the serpentine pattern was clearly etched on the earth below. Still holding the buckle between us, we walked across to the foot of the ladder.

When we reached it, Stuart pressed the buckle into my hand. 'You take it.'

I was about to protest, to say that Stuart should be the one who showed it to everyone else. After all, it was his discovery. But before I could do so, he looked at me with an almost apologetic expression and said, 'Please, darling. I want you to.'

Mrs Pretty's nephew arrived that afternoon. He rode a heavily laden bicycle and weaved his way unsteadily down the gravel path towards the mounds. Piled up behind his saddle were several cylindrical-shaped bags, while two long black tubes were suspended on either side of the back wheel.

His appearance was as chaotic as his bicycle. He had on yellow oilskin trousers and what appeared to be an old golfing jacket. On his head, worn back to front, was a baggy checked cap. He looked just like an Irish tinker.

However, he seemed to know what he was doing. From one of the tubes he took the component parts of a tripod and screwed them together. Kicking out the legs of the tripod, he attached the camera to the platform on the top. Then he ducked down beneath the hood. For the next hour and a half, he took various photographs of the pieces of jewellery, as well as several more of the interior of the ship.

At seven o'clock, we stopped work. I think all of us, Phillips included, felt that to venture any further was somehow inappropriate, even indecent. The tarpaulins were stretched across the ship and secured. Due to the urgency of sending the discoveries down to the British Museum, there was no time to wait for proper containers. Instead, they were packed into sweet bags provided by Robert and then into seed boxes that Mr Jacobs fetched from the kitchen garden.

While this was happening, Phillips came over and said to Stuart, 'A word, if I may.'

'Of course, CW.'

'In private,' said Phillips, with a glance at me.

The two of them walked down to the far end of the ship. From where I was standing they appeared to be having an animated conversation. At least Phillips kept thrusting out his right arm, presumably to lend emphasis to whatever he was saying. Stuart, however, remained quite impassive, not reacting in any way.

They were disturbed – as we all were – by the sound of Mrs Pretty clapping her hands. She beckoned us forward. Phillips and Stuart were the last to come back, their heads still bent together. When we had gathered in a semicircle, Mrs Pretty announced that she would like Mr Brown to carry the seed boxes back to Sutton Hoo House.

'Brown?' said Phillips, looking up sharply.

'Mr Brown,' she confirmed.

Phillips half-dropped one shoulder in acknowledgement. It was at this point that Mr Spooner suggested that no one should carry that much gold about without proper protection. I had no idea if he meant this seriously, but Mrs Pretty evidently thought so.

'A very good point,' she said.

Running off to the stables, Mr Spooner returned with a shotgun. After he had loaded both barrels, we set off. Mr Brown led the way, walking towards the setting sun with three seed boxes resting on his outstretched arms. Alongside him was Mr Spooner, shotgun at the ready in case brigands suddenly sprang out of the bushes. Then came Mrs Pretty and Robert, with Mrs Pretty's nephew wheeling his bicycle in his yellow oilskin trousers. The rest of us brought up the rear.

The next morning I awoke to find Stuart sitting on the side of my bed. I pushed myself up on to my elbows and rubbed my eyes.

'I'm afraid I am going to have to leave you for a day or two, darling,' he said.

'Leave me? What do you mean?'

'I have to go to London. To make arrangements with the British Museum. It's Phillips's idea. I've been turning it over in my head all night, but I can see that he's right. He believes the sooner the treasure is in the BM, the better. Everything we have found so far, along with anything we may find in the future. Plainly that's the place for it, although he anticipates Reid Moir trying to create trouble and claiming it belongs in Ipswich.'

'But surely any finds belong to Mrs Pretty.'

'Ah, well, that's another question altogether.'

'Is it?'

'Absolutely,' he said. 'No doubt there will have to be an inquest of some sort to decide just where it is going to end up. But in the meantime, it's imperative that the finds should be properly examined and catalogued. Phillips has decided that while I am away, he will work with you in the burial chamber. Frank Grimes should be here in a day or two, although there's still been no word from Ward-Perkins or Crawford. Do you mind awfully? I'll be as quick as I can.'

155

'When were you thinking of leaving?'

'Well,' he said, 'there's a train at a quarter to eight.'

It was only then that I noticed his suitcase standing fastened and strapped by the door.

'You'd better be going.'

Stuart stayed where he was, looking down at me. 'I am sorry, darling.' He bent forward and kissed me on the cheek. 'You will be all right with the car, won't you?'

'Of course.'

After he had gone, I remained in bed for a few minutes, flattening the sheet across my stomach, before getting up and dressing.

Driving down towards the estuary, everything looked smaller and more compact than before – the buildings, the streets, even the people. As if they had already shrunk into themselves to try to fend off assault. Beyond Melton and before the fork to Sutton, the road runs straight for several hundred yards. On the left-hand side are fields of sedge grass. On the right, mud flats with a few petrified oaks jutting out of them.

When I reached this stretch, I took my hands off the steering wheel. I did so quite without premeditation or thought to the consequences. The car drifted towards the centre of the road, but stuck to its course.

As it gained speed, it seemed to be straining to take to the air, the stubby black bonnet rising like a prow before me. A cyclist went by in the opposite direction, his head down, unaware of any danger. Still I let the car carry me wherever it wished. I felt no fear, only a sense of being untethered, of hanging suspended between one realm and another. Sometimes I feel that the dead are more alive than the living, and that this life is just a preparation for another one, long gone by.

Just before the fork in the road, I grabbed hold of the steering wheel and swung it around. With a lurch of the chassis, the car rounded the bend, then began climbing the hill that leads to Sutton Hoo House.

Before we went any further with the excavation, Phillips wanted everything we had already found to be properly packaged up in order to be sent down to London. We needed something that was both soft and durable to pack the finds in. Newspaper did not afford enough protection, while straw and strips of burlap were too abrasive. I didn't like to mention it at first – I thought Phillips might scoff at the idea – but when I suggested that the moss in the wood might prove ideal, he agreed it was worth a try.

I volunteered to go to the wood and collect some. As soon as I'd done so, Robert jumped up and said he wanted to come too. After asking me if I minded, Mrs Pretty said that he could. As we set off, Robert slipped his hand into mine. He did so as if it was the most natural thing in the world. I felt the small bunch of his fingers, wrapped in my own.

The moment we stepped into the wood, the air grew cooler. The sunlight, filtered through the leaves, bathed everything in soft green light. We made our way down the slope to where Robert said the moss was at its thickest. This turned out to be at its bottom edge, where the trees were more thinly spaced than they were up above.

One of the men – Mr Spooner – had kindly lent me a pruning knife. It was with surprising ease, as well as an enormous sense of satisfaction, that I was able to hack at the moss, tearing it up by its roots and lifting it out in large squares. These squares, I found, could then be rolled up, or even folded over.

Robert helped me, stacking up the moss into piles. It wasn't long before the two of us had laid waste a large area, turning it from green to brown. As we were working away, Robert told me that he had spent the night with the treasure underneath his bed. His mother had allowed him to keep it there on the understanding that he must not, under any circumstances, open the boxes – a condition he had managed to abide by, but only with the greatest difficulty.

'This is terribly exciting, isn't it?' I said. 'It's just like something out of *Treasure Island*.'

'I don't know. I haven't read *Treasure Island*.'

'I'm sure you'd like it. I certainly did, although it was supposed to be for boys. But then I always preferred boys' books when I was your age. There are lots of pirates and fighting. And a big chest full of treasure.'

'Is there a buried boat?'

'No, but there's a desert island and a man with a long beard. He's called Ben Gunn.'

Together we pulled up another square of moss. A host of black beetles ran about, trying to escape the sudden intrusion of daylight.

'Is it worth a lot of money?' Robert asked.

'Is what worth a lot of money?'

'The treasure, of course.'

'Oh, yes,' I said. 'A great deal of money. I don't think there's any doubt about that.'

'How much money?'

'Well, that might be quite difficult to work out. There's nothing to compare it to, you see.'

'More than a hundred pounds?'

'Definitely more than a hundred pounds,' I told him.

'More than a thousand.'

'I would say definitely more than a thousand too.'

He laughed uncertainly, as if he found this impossible to believe.

'But it's not just its value that's important,' I went on. 'What's even more exciting is that it comes from a time when everyone thought that people had become very primitive. From the Dark Ages. That's why they're called the Dark Ages, you see. Because people were thought to have slid back into darkness. You know about the Romans, don't you, Robert?'

'They had centurions. And legionaries.'

'Exactly. Well, after the Romans left Britain in around AD 400, it was thought that instead of going forward and becoming more clever, people went backwards. They practically became like cavemen again. But this proves they didn't do that at all. If they were capable of making jewellery like the pieces we discovered, they must have been much more clever than anyone ever dreamed of. So, it's very exciting indeed. One of the most exciting things that could ever have happened, in fact.'

'And is it ours?'

'How do you mean?'

'Does it belong to Mummy and me?'

'I don't know,' I said. 'And I'm afraid I don't know how they decide that either.'

'But it was found on Mummy's land, wasn't it?'

'That's right.'

'Well, then, it must belong to us.'

'Yes . . .' I said. 'Yes, it probably does. Why don't we take

some of this moss back? We must have cut more than
enough by now.'

Standing up, I saw an enormous silver object floating in
the sky over Woodbridge. It was roughly cylindrical in
shape. On one end were what looked like fins. The other
end was pointing downwards. While I watched, a second
silver object rose steadily yet clumsily into the air beside it.
When this had reached the same height as the first, it
stopped.

Without my asking, Robert said, 'Barrage balloons. Mr
Jacobs told me about them.'

'What are they for?'

'To stop enemy aircraft. They're supposed to fly into
them and then fall to the ground.'

I couldn't help thinking that the chances of this
happening looked extremely unlikely, although I didn't say
so. I put my arm around Robert's shoulders and together
we stood watching as the two balloons swayed apart and
then bumped into one another, partly crumpling as they
did so.

Picking up armfuls of cut moss, we began to climb back
up the slope. As we did so, I felt suddenly as if the ground
we were walking on was as thin and fragile as the crusted
sand inside the boat. As if it might give way beneath our
feet at any moment and the two of us would tumble into a
black abyss.

Halfway up the slope, we passed a small clearing. A
khaki-coloured bell tent had been pitched in it. The flap
was tied back and the guy ropes fanned out all round.
Inside, I could see a sleeping bag as well as some clothes
scattered about. This, said Robert, was where Mrs Pretty's
nephew, Rory, was staying.

'Isn't he allowed indoors?' I asked, remembering what Phillips had said and wondering if Mrs Pretty had some deep-seated aversion to house guests.

He started to laugh. 'It's not that, silly. He likes being here.'

Apparently Mrs Pretty's nephew preferred sleeping out of doors. Somehow this seemed a very affected thing to want to do, although I didn't say that either.

Slowly, Phillips made his way down the ladder. Every so often he glanced over his shoulder, almost as if he suspected that he was being observed, before lowering himself on to another rung. At the bottom, he stepped off as lightly as he could, hitching his weight up as a woman might do with her skirts. Walking on the balls of his feet, he moved down the ship until he reached the near end of the burial chamber. Once there, he sank to his knees with a sigh.

Without Stuart's presence, the atmosphere had changed more than I would have thought possible. Everything was much more serious, more dour, than before. Even at break times there were no light-hearted moments. Scarcely anyone talked to one another; they just buckled down to their appointed tasks. Having finished moving the spoil heaps from one place to another, the men had now been put to work uncovering the last few rivets in the bow section.

When this was finished, they were able to take the first complete measurements of the ship. It was just under ninety feet from one end to the other. The original ship, however, would have been even longer. The last six feet of the stern end is missing, sheared away. Phillips thought that medieval farmers must have been responsible. It was Mr Brown who suggested the ship might have been deliberately put into the ground at an angle. He believes that the stern protruded above the mound like a great horn, thus ensuring it was clearly visible from the other side of the river. To my surprise, Phillips did not dismiss this theory out of hand, even conceding that it might have some validity to it.

Silently, we continued throughout the afternoon. I was working at the opposite end of the chamber to Phillips. Once in a while, I would look up and see him bent over, his braces stretched and taut. The sun beat down even more fiercely than before.

I was wearing a sleeveless blouse. I could almost see my arms and shoulders turning brown. Practically mahogany. This, though, was no time for vanity. I'd quite stopped caring about my appearance. The only thing that mattered was whatever lay inside the ship.

When Phillips appeared beside me, I gave a start – I couldn't understand how he had got there without my being aware of it. The sides of his nose were shiny with sweat.

'Have you found anything?' he asked.

I showed him a fragment of what I thought was probably a pottery bottle.

'Nothing else?'

I shook my head. Meanwhile, Phillips kept looking at me in an oddly expectant sort of way.

'Have you found anything, Mr Phillips?' I asked.

'I think I have,' he said. 'Come and have a look if you like.'

As I came closer to his end of the chamber, I saw that Phillips had uncovered an edge of pale grey stone. Two flat surfaces were showing – both smooth and at right angles to one another. So far, he had uncovered about eighteen inches of the same straight pumice-coloured, right-angled edge. At either end, the stone disappeared into the sand.

'Whatever this is, he's a big chap,' Phillips said. 'Perhaps we could each start in the middle and work outwards.'

Further clearing revealed that each surface was two inches wide. Once this was done, I moved to my right, following the leading edge along. All the time, I kept expecting to come across a crack or a broken edge. I could not see how such a large object had remained intact – especially if the roof had fallen on top of it. But there was no crack, nor any sign of damage.

Within an hour, the object had grown in length to almost three feet. Still, it was quite uniform and symmetrical, with the edges perfectly smooth. Then, almost immediately, the edges began to taper. I assumed I must be close to one end of it by now. But as quickly as it had tapered off, the stone began to bulge out again. At the same time, the surface became more pitted and undulating. Fortunately, the sand was so dry I was able to brush it away without using the trowel. Phillips too appeared to be nearing the other end. This also tapered and then bulged out again.

Looking across, I saw that Phillips had put on a sudden burst of speed. Sand was flying up on either side of him. But just a few moments later, I noticed that he was no longer brushing. Indeed, he wasn't doing anything at all. I watched and waited for him to carry on, but still he didn't move.

I stood up and crossed over to where he was sitting. When I looked down, I gasped in surprise. There, staring back at me, was a man's face. Its eyes were shut, its mouth pursed and it had a long pointed beard. It looked just like a miniature body lying in the sand. At the same time, though,

I kept expecting its eyes to spring open, as if awakening from a long sleep.

Phillips didn't say anything. He just reached out and stroked the surface of the stone with the tips of his fingers, doing so rather more tenderly than I might have expected.

Soon after resuming, I too uncovered a face. It was identical in size to the first, the shape of an inverted teardrop. This was also bearded – the strands of hair had been picked out in parallel grooves in the stone. But there was a subtle, scarcely definable difference in its expression. Whereas the first face looked penitent, this one looked apprehensive. Fearful of what it might see if it were to open its eyes.

By then Phillips was well on the way to uncovering a second face of his own. Eventually, we had exposed three sides of a long, square-sided piece of stone. At both ends of it, and on each of the surfaces, were bearded faces. All of them with minute variations in expression.

Sliding our trowels underneath the bottom edge of the stone, we inched them along until they met. Next, we dug out a channel so that we could slide our fingers beneath it. Gently we rocked the stone from side to side. When we were as sure as we could be that it wasn't stuck, we lifted each end on a count of three.

It came out quite easily. But the weight was far greater than I had been expecting. Already damp with sweat, my fingers started to slip on the smooth surface. I called to Phillips that we had to put it down. As we did so, the stone rolled over, exposing the fourth – previously buried – surface. Here were two more faces, one on either end.

These faces had different expressions from the others; they might have been showing various forms of contemplation. All eight, however, were perfectly preserved. Phillips and I were on our hands and knees, face to face, with the stone lying between us. Both of us were panting away.

'Do you have any idea what this is?' he asked.

'Some sort of sceptre?'

'A sceptre, yes.' He nodded. 'That's what I thought.'

'Have you ever seen anything like it before?'

'Never!' he said. 'And what's more, nor has anyone else. As far as I know, this has no parallel. Not in European or Scandinavian archaeology at any rate. There have been stone sceptres found in Ireland and Scotland. Only with one face on them, though. Never eight. And never of this size, not remotely.'

He took out his handkerchief and pressed it against his brow. 'You know what this means, don't you?'

I suspected I did know, although at that moment it seemed best not to say so.

'Unless I am very much mistaken,' said Phillips, 'this is the grave of a king.'

I dined alone at the Bull. Literally so – there was no one else in the dining room. The menu offered a choice of gammon or smoked haddock. I ordered the gammon. Although this hadn't been specified on the menu, it came with a fried egg on top. The gammon was sweet and tender, while the egg white slipped down my throat more succulently than an oyster. For pudding, I had a slice of gooseberry pie with cream. It was one of the most delicious meals I had ever eaten.

Afterwards I had planned to go back upstairs. But it wasn't yet ten o'clock and I had no wish to sleep, or read –

still less to listen to the wireless. Unable to think of anything else to do, I went back outside. Although it was dark, the air was still warm. Estuary smells drifted up the hill: a mix of gutted fish and baked mud. Several dogs ran about in a proprietorial fashion, as though darkness had conferred a kind of ownership upon them. On the market square pub doors were open. Puddles of light spilled on to the road.

As I walked along the pavement up to the Shire Hall, three men came out of one of the pubs. Judging by the disjointed way they moved, all three of them had had too much to drink.

They walked towards me. When they were a few feet away they stopped, blocking the pavement. I could see the men quite clearly now, could see how young they were.

'Fancy a nightcap, darling?' said one.

The other two began to laugh. Encouraged by their response, the first man went on, 'Seems a shame for a lovely girl like you to be all on her own. Haven't you got a sweetheart to cuddle?'

I had stopped now. I couldn't go past them without stepping into the road.

'Why don't you let one of us oblige?' the man said, his confidence growing. 'There's always Jackie here. He can be a bit daft when he's had a few, but he's very gentle. So I've heard, anyway.'

I wanted to tell him not to be so stupid, to stand aside and let me pass. But I could feel myself flushing, turning bright red. Even the roots of my hair felt as if they were on fire.

'Or there's Vincent,' he said. 'He's a right terror, though, when he fixes his mind on something. Aren't you, Vince?

Or there's me, of course. Now, which of us lucky lads would you prefer?'

I felt paralysed with embarrassment. Rooted to the spot. As though I'd been pegged out for people to laugh and jeer at. Turning around, I began to walk away, my arms crossed over my chest. From behind, I could hear the men's laughter – no longer embarrassed, but more full-throated than before. The laughter followed me all the way back to the hotel.

When I opened the door to my room, I saw a telegram lying on the floor.

CHAOS HERE STOP EVERYTHING TAKING LONGER
THAN EXPECTED STOP BACK SOON AS POSSIBLE STOP
ALL LOVE STUART STOP

Frank Grimes turned up the next day. He was a rabbity-looking man in a neatly pressed navy-blue boiler suit, who bowed at me formally, like a Chinese mandarin. Phillips said that he and I should work together. I imagined that Grimes's arrival meant that Phillips would go back to supervising operations from outside the ship. However, this did not happen.

During the morning Grimes uncovered a tangled mass of purplish metal. It was roughly circular, almost spherical in shape. He lifted it out, took it up the ladder and laid it on the grass. It looked even more bizarre sitting there than it had done in the trench, like a battered collection of old cooking utensils.

From the top of the bank, I saw that harvesting had started in the field next door. Two horses were pulling a reaping machine through the ripened barley. Its blades rotated slowly as it kicked up a cloud of dust and chaff. Every few yards the horses would stop for some blockage to be cleared or for a stone to be shifted. Then the man sitting on the reaper would set the horses going again with a flick of the reins.

For some reason Phillips's mood had changed for the worse. He could hardly bring himself to wish me good morning and seemed no more communicative with anyone else. In the afternoon, I went looking for him, intending to ask what he wanted Mr Grimes and myself to do next. After finishing one side of the chamber, I thought it best to check with him before proceeding further.

I found him at the bottom of the bank. He was standing with his hands on his hips, shouting at Mrs Pretty's nephew.

'Haven't I told you before that you can't simply wander around taking your photographs as you see fit! Sticking your equipment into the soil and leaving great footprints everywhere!'

This struck me as being unfair. However scruffily dressed he might be, Mrs Pretty's nephew had taken care to be as discreet as possible, always asking people if he was getting in their way before taking a photograph. As for leaving footprints, this seemed unlikely as he wore plimsolls. Battered black plimsolls it was true, but plimsolls none the less.

'I will not deny that it is useful to have a photographic record of the excavation,' Phillips went on at a similar volume to before. 'I will not deny that. But in future, I must insist you ask my permission before taking any pictures. Have I made myself understood?'

Mrs Pretty's nephew held his head on one side and his

cheeks sucked in, revealing the blades of his cheekbones. He looked oddly studious, as if he had never come across anyone quite like Phillips before and didn't want to waste the opportunity of examining him at close quarters. Briefly, his eyes flickered over Phillips's shoulder to where I was standing and then back again.

Phillips, meanwhile, had not finished yet. If anything, he appeared to be gearing up for another assault. Before he could do so, I stepped forward and said, 'I wonder if I might have a word, Mr Phillips.'

He didn't bother to turn around. 'Not now. Just wait until I have finished.' Once again, he prepared to continue.

'Where would you like me to wait?' I asked. 'Here? Or shall I go back to the chamber and wait there?'

At this, he did spin round, doing so with surprising agility. 'Wait wherever you like, for heaven's sake! Oh . . . never mind. I'm through here anyway.'

He walked off, brushing past me as he did so. I suppose I might have followed, but there didn't seem much point. When he had gone, Mrs Pretty's nephew turned his attention to me. There was a slight twitch on one side of his mouth. I couldn't tell if this was a nervous reaction or suppressed laughter.

'I should keep your distance, if I were you,' he said. 'I'm in the doghouse.'

'So I gather.'

'What's got into Phillips?'

'I don't know. He seems to be having a bad day.'

'You can say that again.'

He rubbed his hand back and forth through his hair several times, as if trying to eradicate the memory of Phillips. Then he stopped and gave a rueful grin. 'Oh, well,

I dare say it'll blow over. I know these are not exactly ideal circumstances, but we've never really met. I'm Rory – Rory Lomax.'

'Peggy Piggott.'

We shook hands.

'I'm just staying here for a few days,' he said.

'I know . . . I've seen your tent,' I added stupidly.

He was rather taken aback by this, even embarrassed. 'Ah, yes, well, I'm not really camping out, you know. I mean, I am, but I can always take a bath in the house. And they do my laundry for me. So I'm a bit of a fraud really.' He paused, as if to consider this idea further. 'Mind you, there's nothing to beat sleeping out of doors. Not at this time of year at any rate. Lying in my tent and listening to the nightingales.'

'Nightingales?' I exclaimed in disbelief.

'Well, most of them have gone by now, of course. There are still some around, though. Why? Haven't you heard them?'

'Only on the wireless,' I said.

He was thoroughly confused now. 'On the wireless?' he repeated dazedly.

'It really doesn't matter . . .'

As we were standing there, Grateley, the butler, came over and asked if we would like some lemonade.

'What do you say?' said Rory Lomax. 'I could do with some.'

After we had taken a couple of glasses from the tray, he suggested we sit down for a moment. I could see no reason to go back to work immediately – not with Phillips in this sort of mood – so we went off and sat in the deep velvety shadows beneath the yew trees.

'Now,' he said, 'what's all this about hearing nightingales on the wireless?'

'Oh . . . it's rather a long story, I'm afraid.'

'I don't mind.'

I wished I had kept my mouth shut, of course. However, I didn't want to appear rude, so I had little choice but to proceed. 'There's a cellist called Beatrice Harrison,' I began. 'She was Sir Edward Elgar's favourite cellist – although that's not really relevant here . . . Anyway, during the summer she liked to practise her cello out of doors. In her spinney. One evening she was playing a piece of music when she heard a nightingale singing along with her. At first, she thought it must be a strange coincidence. But just to make sure, she started playing a scale. And the nightingale accompanied her.'

'Are you quite sure about this?' Rory Lomax asked.

'Absolutely positive,' I told him. 'The next night she tried again and the same thing happened. And the next – just the same. Miss Harrison was so excited that she went to see Lord Reith at the BBC. She thought the BBC might be interested in recording it, you see. But Lord Reith didn't think it was a good idea. Not at first. He thought it might discourage people from actually going out to listen to nightingales. But Miss Harrison persuaded him that there were lots of people living in places where there was no chance of them ever hearing a nightingale, and so in the end he agreed.'

I stopped. Rory Lomax was looking at me with exactly the same sucked-in, studious expression with which he'd been regarding Charles Phillips.

'Go on,' he said.

'Do you really want me to?'

171

'Oh, I'm absolutely positive.'

'Well . . . the next time Miss Harrison went to practise outside there were microphones and amplifiers in place. She started playing as usual. The trouble was, nothing happened. First, she tried some Dvořák. That had worked in the past. Then Elgar, and finally "Danny Boy". But still nothing. There wasn't a sound, apart from her cello, of course. Everyone was very jumpy by now – going to all that trouble for nothing. And then, just as they were all getting ready to go, the nightingale started to sing. It carried on for the next fifteen minutes, its voice rising and falling along with Miss Harrison's cello. And that wasn't all – people who had been listening to the broadcast in their gardens reported that other nightingales had also started singing along. Afterwards Miss Harrison received more than 50,000 letters of appreciation.'

When I had finished Rory Lomax didn't say anything, not for a while. Indeed he seemed so taken aback by this story that I began to wonder if he was putting it on.

'But that's wonderful,' he said at last.

'Yes, it was . . . It was wonderful . . .'

The silence between us was broken by a loud click. The sound came from Grimes's tangle of purple metal. It was still on the grass, where he had put it earlier. Only now it had sprung open. Apparently warmed and unlocked by the sun, the metal casing had split apart.

We looked down in astonishment. Inside, was a nest of silver bowls, one inside the other. There were eight in all, each decorated with a cruciform design. Apart from some slight corrosion around the edges, they were in mint condition. If anything, they were even brighter and shinier than the gold we had found. As we laid the bowls out along the top of the bank, sunlight swirled around the inside of their surfaces and bounced back at us.

The next day preparations began for Mrs Pretty's sherry party. The men were put to work levelling off the largest of the spoil heaps – in order to give guests an elevated vantage point from which they would be able to look down into the ship. They also scythed the grass beside the shepherd's hut so that the Woodbridge Silver Band would have a level surface on which to play their instruments.

I assumed that these intrusions would infuriate Charles Phillips, but he didn't react at all. This, I realized, was his way of dealing with trouble; he simply hung up an invisible curtain between himself and whatever displeased him. The more something displeased him, the more impenetrable the curtain became. At the same time, he appeared to be quite unaware of his own inconsistency; one mood simply replaced another like a series of eclipses, with each one obliterating its predecessor.

There was no doubt, though, that the preparations hampered our work. Already we were desperately short of manpower – still there was no sign of either Mr Crawford or Mr Ward-Perkins.

None the less, we did make one more significant find. To begin with Phillips thought that he had uncovered a shield. But as he went on it became clear that this was an enormous dish, almost two feet in diameter. Made of silver like the bowls, it was badly dented on one side, yet otherwise unmarked. The centre of the dish was decorated with an eight-pointed star and on the rim were two stamps. One was hexagonal and consisted of lettering. The other was oval. Within the oval was the image of a veiled and haloed woman.

Phillips pointed at the stamps. 'These, as you may or may not be aware, are control stamps of the Emperor Anastasius I. Anastasius, of course, being ruler of the Byzantine Empire from AD 491 to 518. Incredible, isn't it? For centuries, everyone thought these people could barely make a club to beat each other over the head with. Now we find that their trading routes stretched as far as Constantinople.'

At lunchtime, Phillips lay against a tree trunk in his shirtsleeves, his legs stretched out in front of him. Mr Grimes was also lying down, with his hands behind his head. While the rest of us became covered in mud and dust as a result of working in the chamber, his boiler suit was always immaculate. Mr Jacobs, Mr Brown and Mr Spooner were sitting by themselves, a little distance away.

Robert was also there, wandering about distractedly and looking upset. His cheeks, I saw, were wet with tears. When I asked him what the matter was, he said that he had lost one of his roller-skates. I tried to reassure him that it was bound to turn up sooner or later.

'How do you know?' he asked.

'I don't know for certain,' I said. 'I just think it probably will.'

I would have been perfectly happy having lunch on my own, but no sooner had I settled down than Mrs Pretty called me over. She was sitting in her wicker chair with her nephew, Rory, on a blanket at her feet. I sat beside him on the blanket.

'I do hope your husband will be back for the sherry party,' Mrs Pretty said.

'I'm sure he will make it if he possibly can.'

'It is so good of you both to come here. It can hardly have been the start to married life that you were anticipating.'

'Believe me, Mrs Pretty, I would not have missed this for the world.'

After we had finished eating, Rory went off to take some more photographs while the burial chamber was deserted. I was about to go myself when Mrs Pretty said, 'My dear . . . I wonder if I could ask you something. I would have asked Mr Phillips, except that he seems a little preoccupied today.'

'Of course.'

Mrs Pretty had not eaten anything, at least not while I had been there. None the less, she touched her napkin to her lips before continuing. 'Does it not strike you as strange that you have not found a body? The tomb – plainly it is a tomb – contains the grave goods of someone of great importance. And yet there is no sign of whoever was buried there.'

She was quite right, of course. It was strange that we had found no sign of a body. To begin with, Phillips had been convinced that it was only a matter of time. However, as the excavation had gone on, he seemed less and less willing to discuss the subject. From this I concluded that he was as puzzled by the absence of a body as everyone else.

I explained that this might not be a grave at all, but a memorial. Possibly for someone lost at sea, or else killed in battle.

'You mean, there might never have been a body at all?'

'That is a possibility,' I admitted.

'But if there is a body, might it still be there?'

'Oh, yes. It's much too early to give up hope.'

'Thank you, my dear,' she said. 'That was all I wanted to know.'

*

There was no further word from Stuart that day. Only after returning to the hotel did I remember that I had better give some thought to what I was going to wear for Mrs Pretty's sherry party. Not that I had any real choice: the only possibility was my going-away outfit. On Stuart's insistence, this had been made especially for me by Mr Molyneux of Bond Street. Both the jacket and the skirt were in russet-coloured silk, while the buttons were all ormolu.

But when I put it on and stood in front of the mirror, I was appalled to see a brawny farm-girl staring back at me. I blinked, hoping she might disappear. Only she didn't disappear; she stayed stubbornly in place. My shoulders appeared to have broadened and my wrists to have thickened. My hands were as rough as a navvy's. There was a sharp V of suntanned skin on my chest that looked ridiculous with the hooped neck of the jacket. My only consolation, I thought, was that at least Stuart would be spared from seeing me like this.

It had rained during the night. The grass squelched beneath my feet as I walked out to the mounds. We brushed the water away from the edges of the tarpaulins and mopped up the residue with foul-smelling sponges. The men had already set up rows of wooden chairs below the levelled-off spoil heap. There were far more chairs than I had expected; I counted close to 100.

From the beginning it was plain that we were unlikely to be able to do much work that day. At two o'clock, Phillips called a halt and said that we should all go and prepare ourselves for the party. Mrs Pretty had offered me the use of a bedroom to change in, but I felt more comfortable doing so in the shepherd's hut – somehow I felt that a more dramatic transformation might be expected if I changed in the house.

Robert stood guard outside to make sure that no one barged in. Around my neck I wore a gold and ruby necklace that had belonged to my grandmother. I hoped it might make my sunburn less evident. By the time I emerged, trestle tables had been erected at the foot of the spoil heap and covered with white tablecloths. Sherry bottles and glasses stood waiting, along with teacups and saucers. Resplendent in their uniforms, the Woodbridge Silver Band unpacked their instruments and set out their sheet music. Rabbits hopped unconcernedly about between the metal legs of the music stands.

'Ready?' said Charles Phillips.

He had changed into a fawn-coloured suit and was wearing a larger bow tie than usual, along with a matching handkerchief that spilled from his breast pocket.

'Now,' he said, 'I am sure I don't need to tell you that secrecy is the key.'

'Secrecy?'

'If news of this gets out we'll have all sorts of people swarming round here. Journalists and the like – dreadful people. No doubt you will be asked no end of fatuous questions. Just don't tell them any more than you have to, is that clear?'

'Quite clear,' I said.

'Good girl.'

At five o'clock, the conductor tapped his baton and raised his hands, whereupon the band launched into 'A Londonderry Air'. Soon afterwards, the first guests arrived, making their way out from Sutton Hoo House in small groups. As the leading group came closer, Phillips muttered, 'God help us.'

The group consisted of three men and a woman. Two of the men as well as the woman were wearing tweed suits, while the third man had on a suit made from a similar fawn material to that worn by Phillips. However, this suit was of a considerably better cut than his. From the way the material flowed as he walked along, it appeared to have been sculpted to his body. When the third man saw Phillips, he stopped for a moment, then came forward more slowly than before.

'Good afternoon, Mr Phillips,' he said.

'Good afternoon, Reid Moir,' said Phillips. 'May I introduce Mrs Peggy Piggott? This is Mr Reid Moir and Mr Maynard. From Ipswich Museum,' he added.

'How do you do?' said Mr Reid Moir smoothly. 'May I introduce my friends, Sir Joseph and Lady Veevers. This is Charles Phillips, from Selwyn College, Cambridge . . . Sir Joseph, as I'm sure you know, is the Lord Lieutenant of Suffolk.'

'A Selwyn man?' said Sir Joseph after we had shaken hands. 'Do you know Wagstaff? From Emmanuel?'

'I don't believe I do,' said Phillips.

'A. P. Wagstaff?'

Phillips shook his head.

'A. P. Wagstaff, the palaeontologist?' Sir Joseph pressed on.

Again Phillips shook his head. Clearly he had no intention of budging. Sir Joseph seemed unsure how to proceed. He continued to regard Phillips with a puzzled frown as Reid Moir said, 'I understand you are favouring us with a speech.'

'A speech? How delightful,' said Lady Veevers.

'A brief address,' Phillips conceded. 'Nothing more.'

'I trust you will be paying due credit to Ipswich Museum in your brief address,' said Reid Moir.

Phillips made no reply to this.

'And of course Sir Joseph and Lady Patience are very much looking forward to seeing the finds. As we all are.'

'Joseph and I have been able to think of little else for days,' said Lady Patience.

Phillips turned to her. 'Then I fear you will be disappointed.'

'I – I don't think I understand.'

'Are you saying the finds are no longer here?' said Reid Moir.

'No,' said Phillips. 'I'm not saying that. Some pieces are still here. However, we have decided not to show them, not to members of the public.'

Reid Moir took a step forward. 'May I remind you that Sir Joseph and Lady Patience are my personal guests,' he said, speaking quietly and almost furtively. 'Also that there would not even have been an excavation if it had not been for Ipswich Museum.'

'Possibly so. None the less, Mrs Pretty is very concerned about security. Rightly so, in my opinion.'

'Now, look here, Phillips . . .' said Reid Moir, taking another step forward.

Phillips looked down on him with detached interest, rather as if Reid Moir was about to attempt an ascent of his shirt front.

At that moment other guests arrived. Unaware that anything was amiss, they started to talk to Phillips. As they did so, Reid Moir steered Sir Joseph and Lady Veevers off towards the mounds. I also took the opportunity to slip away. Already people were lining the edges and peering down into the ship. Shielding their eyes from the sun with one hand, they reached for sandwiches and cakes with the other.

The band, meanwhile, played a selection of hymns and subdued marching songs. After half an hour or so, following prompting from Grateley and other members of staff, everyone sat down for Phillips's address. I didn't sit down, but stood off to one side. The band stopped playing.

Phillips strode out in front of the chairs. He waited until there was absolute quiet and then announced, 'Due to the risk of landslides, we have decided that no one can be allowed up on to the grandstand area.'

There was a groan of disappointment at this. Phillips ignored it. Keeping one hand in his jacket pocket, he proceeded to give a cursory and remarkably undramatic account of the discovery of the ship.

Soon after he had begun talking, people started to shift about on their chairs. For some reason, Phillips's voice sounded unusually faint. Only guests in the first few rows were able to hear anything. Matters were not helped by a high-pitched buzzing sound that was coming from overhead.

I glanced up.

There was an aeroplane high in the sky, sunlight glinting off its wings. Phillips continued to talk. His lips were moving anyway, although nothing seemed to be emerging. 'Please speak up,' people shouted from the back. Then, more plaintively, 'We can't hear anything!'

Still Phillips carried on, just as inaudibly as before. The buzzing sound grew steadily louder. Then all at once it turned from an annoying distraction into a high-pitched mechanical scream.

I looked up again.

Now the aeroplane was pointing vertically at the ground, wrapped in this stream of air. I could see the blades of its propeller spinning round. Also the lines of rivets along its fuselage. All around me I was aware of people diving for cover. But I stayed where I was. I couldn't look away. The hood of the cockpit was pulled back. There was a man's head inside. Shiny and brown, like an enormous nut.

Air beat against my cheeks, pulling my hair back. The screaming seemed to fill every part of my body, shaking everything up. Thrilling and appalling me at the same time. I felt a blow against my side. My feet were swept from under me. Twisting round as I fell, I saw the aeroplane skimming across the tops of the mounds, pulling up just in time to clear the trees. When it had gone, two plumes of black exhaust remained hanging in the air.

No one moved for a few moments. Then a voice said, 'Are you all right?'

I looked over to where Rory Lomax was lying. Dimly and resentfully, I realized he must have pushed me over.

'Are you all right?' he repeated.

'What happened?'

'Some damn fool showing off, I expect. Either that, or he was trying to hear Phillips's speech.'

I stood up and brushed myself down.

'Look,' he said. 'You've grazed your knee.'

'It's perfectly all right.'

'But it's bleeding.'

I looked down and saw a small smear of blood just below my right knee.

'Hardly.'

'Here, let me.' Rory Lomax had already started unwinding a cream silk scarf from around his neck.

'Please,' I said. 'It's not necessary. Besides, I have a hanky.'

I wiped the blood away – there really was very little.
Rory Lomax stayed where he was, still holding his silk scarf
in both hands. Everyone else was standing up now. Some
were still brushing themselves down, others talking
excitedly to one another.

The band cleaned off their instruments and prepared to
start playing again. It was at this point that I saw Mr Jacobs
running towards me. He ran straight past, continuing
through the crowd until he reached Charles Phillips. Once
there, he stopped and began talking to him. He hadn't been
doing so for long when Phillips raised his head.

I followed his gaze. Four people were making their way
up the side of the levelled spoil heap. Reid Moir was in
front, with Sir Joseph and Lady Veevers behind him.
Maynard brought up the rear. As soon as he saw them,
Phillips strode over to the foot of the spoil heap. 'Will you
come down?' he bellowed.

Reid Moir ignored him. He kept going until he had
reached the platform. Once there, he stood defiantly,
holding on to the guard rail with both hands. As we
watched, the other three joined him, looking rather less
defiant.

'You must come down,' Phillips shouted.

'This is the Lord Lieutenant of Suffolk,' Reid Moir
retorted. 'And Lady Veevers.'

'I couldn't care less who they are,' Phillips shouted back.
'Do you understand? I want everyone back down here this
instant!'

From the bottom of the spoil heap people looked on in
surprise. Plainly wishing to avoid a confrontation, Sir
Joseph and Lady Veevers immediately started to come back

down. They were soon followed by Maynard. But Reid Moir stayed where he was, presumably until he felt he had made his point. Then he too came back down. On reaching ground level, he marched up to Phillips. 'You have ordered me off Suffolk soil,' he said. This, it seemed, was the worst insult of all.

'I made it perfectly clear that no one was to go up there,' Phillips told him. 'Yet you chose to disregard my words. Leaving me with no choice but to ask you to come down.'

'Ask?' repeated Reid Moir incredulously. '*Ask?*'

He stalked off, with Maynard following. Left on their own, Sir Joseph and Lady Veevers stood about looking embarrassed and then did their best to melt back into the crowd.

'Just as well this is England, isn't it?' said Rory Lomax.

'What do you mean?'

'Give this lot machine guns and they'd be as bad as Chicago gangsters.'

We began to walk through the guests. I felt like one of the apostles from a medieval wall painting whose feet hang in the air, limp and white, to show how they're being blown about by divine winds.

'Good afternoon, madam,' said a voice.

A man was standing in front of me. He was wearing a somewhat ancient but sturdily fashioned suit, a tie dotted with small green crests and a trilby hat. In the corner of his mouth there was a pipe clamped between his teeth.

It took me a few moments to realize who he was. 'Mr Brown . . . Forgive me, I didn't recognize you.'

Mr Brown didn't seem in the least put out. He grinned and said, 'That's because I've put my make-up on.'

Beside him was a woman dressed in a black coat and hat.

Stiff coils of hair jutted out from under her hat. Her high, almost inflamed colour added to her rather wild appearance. This, said Mr Brown, was his wife, May.

She extended a hand. For a few minutes we talked about the excavation and I took the opportunity to tell Mrs Brown what an invaluable help her husband had been.

'You see, Basil?' she said. 'At least someone realizes.'

'May, now that's enough.'

Mrs Brown took no notice. 'My Basil may be self-taught and not have the right letters after his name,' she went on. 'Even so, that's no reason to treat him like he's all sappy in the head. The trouble is, he's too trusting, you see. He takes people at their word. I've told him he shouldn't, but it makes no difference, none at all. Does it, Basil?'

Just as I was wondering if Mrs Brown might have had a little too much sherry to drink, Mr Reid Moir came towards us. He still looked shaken after his encounter with Phillips. There was hardly any trace of his former emollience. However, any hopes he might have had of having his equanimity restored were soon dashed.

Mrs Brown waited until he was standing beside her before announcing triumphantly, 'And here's the man responsible!'

'May!' said Mr Brown again.

'No, Basil, no. I will be heard. I'm not saying Mr Reid Moir's any worse than the others. All I'm saying is that everyone is out to hog the glory for themselves, when the man who found this ship in the first place and who made a proper excavation every bit as good as anyone else could have done is my Basil.'

Reid Moir's only reaction to this was to brush the lapel of his jacket, very deliberately, with the index finger of his

right hand. In the silence that followed, Mr Brown took
hold of his wife's elbow, presumably intending to lead her
away. But their exit was effectively blocked by the arrival
of Mrs Pretty and Robert. As far as I was aware, Mrs Pretty
had not heard Mrs Brown's outburst, yet she seemed to
read the situation immediately and to realize just what was
required.

'You must be Mr Brown's wife, May,' she said. 'I have
heard so much about you.'

'You have?' said Mrs Brown, clearly taken aback by this.

'Indeed. And I know how much Mr Brown has been
missing you while he has been here.'

'He has?' said Mrs Brown, even more taken aback now.

Mrs Pretty's gaze passed over each of us in turn, pausing
briefly on her nephew and myself. 'I do hope you have all
enjoyed yourselves this afternoon.'

'Very much so,' I said.

'I am glad . . . I think it has gone as well as could have
been expected.' Her eyebrows rose fractionally. 'Bar the
odd intrusion.'

Unusually for him, Robert stood quite still by his
mother's side, not saying anything.

'Hello there, young man,' said Mr Brown.

Robert looked up at him. He seemed to be coming to a
decision. 'Hello, Mr Brown,' he said.

People were already beginning to leave. They came to say
their goodbyes to Mrs Pretty, queuing up to thank her for
her hospitality, before drifting away. Lengthening shadows
undulated across the cropped grass. It wasn't until most of
the guests had gone that Rory asked, 'What are you
planning to do now?'

'I don't know,' I told him. 'I hadn't really thought.'

'It's just that I wondered if you had any plans.'

'Plans?'

'For later. I thought perhaps you might like to go for a walk in the woods. To see if we can hear a nightingale. I can't promise anything. As I said before, it's a bit late in the year for them now. But you'd be very welcome to come along, if you like.'

'Yes,' I said. 'I would like that.'

'You'd have to change first, of course. I mean, you couldn't possibly go tramping about like that.'

'Couldn't I?'

'Absolutely not. You're far too smart. I should bring a sweater too, if I were you. It can turn quite chilly after the sun has gone in. Why don't we meet outside the squash court at, say, eight o'clock?'

'At eight, then,' I said.

When I arrived at the squash court, Rory was already waiting. He was wearing a long herringbone overcoat I had not seen before, along with his Irish tinker's cap, worn the right way round this time.

'Hello,' he said, and held up a thermos flask. 'I've brought along some coffee to keep us going.'

There was a cinder path that skirted the house and crossed the top of a meadow – it must have been a meadow once, although now it was choked with bracken. Running along our left-hand side was a white paling fence. I smelled the sweet, louche smell of gorse, then honeysuckle, and then, just as intensely, wild garlic. The smell was so strong that someone might have rubbed their hands together and opened them right under my nose.

Rory turned on a torch.

A wand of light illuminated our way. At the end of the cinder path was a stile leading into a wood. When we were on the other side he said, 'Everything becomes much steeper from now on. Be careful where you put your feet – there are rabbit holes all over the place. And do remember to watch out for brambles, won't you?'

We descended through the trees, our footfalls giving out muffled thumps. The torch beam swung about. I couldn't see the river – not from here – but there was a cool breeze blowing up the slope. The smell was quite different now, although almost as strong. Dry sand overlaid with the tang of pine.

I stumbled and, without meaning to, cried out.

'Here,' said Rory. 'Take my hand. Just for this bit. Until it becomes flatter.'

I scarcely hesitated before putting my hand in his. Yet once I had done so, I felt as if my entire being had become concentrated in my fingers. After we had been going for a few minutes the ground levelled off into a narrow shelf that ran along the side of the bank.

'Why don't we try here?' he said, and released my hand.

We both sat down. The ground was covered with dead leaves. They were quite dry – it was like sitting on a mound of kapok.

'Cup of coffee?'

Although I didn't want any, it seemed churlish to refuse after Rory had taken the trouble to bring it. He poured out a cup and passed it to me. The coffee tasted vile, like burnt biscuits, but I drank it anyway.

'Aren't you having any?' I asked.

'There's only the one cup. I forgot to bring another one. Stupid of me.'

'Have some of this.'

'No, no. Honestly.'

'But I insist,' I said, and handed the cup to him.

He drank what was left and then poured himself some more. When he had finished, he pushed his cap back and turned off the torch.

'All we can do is wait and hope we'll be lucky,' he said. 'Most of the nightingales have paired off by now. There are just the odd few left. The unlucky ones. Mind you, they say that desperation makes them sing all the harder.'

We sat in silence. Rory leaned back with his head resting against the trunk of a tree. I was sitting up with my arms clasped around my knees. Through the trees I could see narrow streaks of silver where the moonlight hit the water.

After a while he said, 'Do you know this part of the world?'

He sounded so solemn that I almost burst out laughing.

'No,' I said. 'I've never been here. Not before.'

'The first time I came here, I didn't think much of it. All flat and featureless. When people said how much they liked it, I couldn't understand what they meant. But it rather steals up on you. Perhaps it's the lack of variety that makes you notice things more.'

'What sort of things?'

'Oh, I don't know really. Small things. Things that might otherwise pass you by.'

'Where were you brought up?' I asked.

'Essex,' he said. 'Near Chelmsford. Do you know it?'

I shook my head.

'That's pretty too, of course. But in a different sort of way. They grow a lot of fruit round there. For jam,' he added, almost as solemnly as before.

'Jam?'

'That's right.'

A few stars had appeared above the tops of the trees. Down below, the foliage was too dense for any light to penetrate. Everything was quite black.

'What about you?' he said.

'What about me?'

'Where do your people come from?'

'I'm not really sure if I have any people,' I said.

'How do you mean?'

There's something about the darkness that invites confidences, of course. Or draws them forth without one realizing. Almost before I was aware of doing so, I found myself telling him how my father had died when I was very young. And how the four of us – my two sisters, my brother and myself – were taken in by my uncle and aunt.

'Did your father die in the war?' Rory asked.

'No,' I said. 'No, he didn't. He drowned. We went on holiday to Cornwall. He had petit mal. He'd had it since he was a boy. He must have had an attack while he was swimming. I saw him being pulled out of the water. They tried to give him mouth-to-mouth resuscitation, but I think he was probably dead by then.'

'That must have been very hard for you.'

'It was a long time ago now.'

'But what about your mother?'

Closing my eyes, I felt as if I had been transported to the top of a cliff. A chalk cliff, high above the sea, with a great wilderness of blue laid out before me.

'My mother ran off with an army doctor a few months before my father died,' I said.

Rory didn't reply, not immediately. I wondered if he disapproved – either of my frankness or my circumstances.

'Did she die soon after that?'

'No,' I said, 'she didn't die.'

'I don't understand.'

'She just didn't want to see us any more.'

'You mean you've never had any contact with your mother?'

'Never. But I believe she lives in London.'

'I see . . . And how did your uncle and aunt treat you?'

'They were very kind,' I said automatically. But even as I was saying it I found myself remembering the swing door that separated their part of the house from ours and the reproving shush it made whenever it closed. I remembered, too, waking up and seeing a charity box on our bedroom mantelpiece. A cast-iron figure of a little black boy with 'For Foundlings' printed on the base. I always assumed this must refer to us.

'Are you all right?' he said. 'You're shivering. Here, let me put my coat around your shoulders.'

'No, please . . .'

'But it's no trouble.'

He draped his coat around me. As hard as I could, I tried to stop this jumping and twitching in my veins.

'Why don't you tell me how you first became interested in archaeology?'

'You can't possibly want to know that.'

'I wouldn't have asked if I didn't want to know.'

And so I told him how, when I had been a child, a friend of my uncle's had come for lunch one day. I couldn't have been more than five or six at the time. A keen numismatist, he had given me a coin that he told me dated from the time of Augustus. I knew about Caesar Angustus from Bible reading. At least I knew that Christ had taken out a coin

and told his disciples to render unto Caesar the things that
were Caesar's and unto God the things that were God's.

'I don't know why exactly,' I said. 'I don't think it was
anything the man said, not directly, but I became convinced
that the coin I'd been given was the same coin that Christ
had showed the disciples. It made such a big impression on
me, I can't tell you. For years afterwards I used to take the
coin out and marvel at being able to touch it myself. I used
to think it would bring me luck.'

'And did it?'

'I'm not sure. I suppose it must have done.'

'Then what happened?'

With no prompting at all, I told him how my uncle and
aunt had insisted that I become a debutante. How at one of
the balls I'd attended I had met a young man who said that
he was going off to excavate an Iron Age village in Bosnia.
At the end of the evening, I'd asked if I could go with him.

'What did he say to that?'

'He was a bit taken aback at first, but after a while he
said yes.'

'You mean you went off on your own with this person
that you'd only just met?'

'It was all perfectly above board, I assure you. We were
out there for a month – we both had the most marvellous
time. Then, when I came back, I applied to study
archaeology at University College.'

'How did your uncle and aunt react?'

'Oh, they were absolutely furious. They thought I had let
the family down. And myself, of course. On my twenty-first
birthday, my uncle told the maid to set my place on his
right-hand side. He said I was no longer a member of the
household. I was only a guest. The next morning I left. I'm

sure they were relieved to see the back of me. I can't really blame them. I was very troublesome, you see. I always have been. Even as a child, I never stopped asking questions. That was bad enough, but what made it even worse was that their answers never seemed to satisfy me.'

Rory gave a shout of laughter.

'There,' I said, relieved to have finished. 'That's all there is to me.'

'I'm sure it isn't.'

'What do you mean?'

'There must be lots of things you haven't told me.'

'About what?'

'Well, for instance, you haven't told me how you met your husband.'

'Stuart?'

'Yes,' he said, amused. 'Stuart.'

'He was my tutor,' I told him. 'At the university.'

'And did you know straight away?'

'Did I know what straight away?'

He paused. 'It's none of my business,' he said.

'Tell me. I don't mind.'

'I just wondered if you knew straight away that you wanted to marry him.'

'Not straight away, no,' I said. 'But we had a lot in common. Shared interests are very important, don't you think?'

'I wouldn't know.'

'Why not?'

'Because it's never happened to me. I wish it had, but it hasn't. Not yet anyway. Still, I live in hope . . .'

We sat in silence. I rested my head against the bark of the tree. The only sounds were the occasional rustle in the undergrowth and the odd splash from the river. I could no longer see Rory. I could only hear him breathing.

After we had sat there for a while I said, 'Now it's your turn.'

'Oh, there's nothing much to tell. Nothing as dramatic anyway.'

'Let's see, I already know where you were brought up. Where they make jam. Why don't you tell me what made you become interested in photography?'

'I suppose – I suppose it seemed a way of trying to fix moments as they went past. To try to capture them and give them some physical existence. Stop them from being lost for ever. Not that it necessarily works like that.'

'Doesn't it?'

'Not really. For instance, do you know why there aren't any people in photographs of Victorian London? Take a look some time. In early pictures, the streets are completely deserted. Obviously, they weren't deserted. It was just that the plates needed to be exposed for such a long time that people – moving people – didn't register at all. Occasionally, you can see a misty outline, but nothing more. It's a strange thought, isn't it? All these ghostly, transparent people making no lasting impression . . .' He broke off. 'I don't know if that makes any sense.'

'Yes. Of course it does.'

'Really?'

'It makes perfect sense. That's why I wanted to study archaeology. So much of life just slips by, and with so little to show for it. I suppose I wanted to make sense of what does endure.'

Rory had rolled over towards me. I could see the pale oval of his face close to mine. 'That's it!' he said. 'That's it exactly! Especially now. I mean, what do you think people are likely to find of us in 2,000 years' time? Do you think they might find this thermos and wonder who it belonged to? Who drank from this cup? And even if they do wonder, they'll never know. Not about us. Who we were. What we were thinking and feeling at the time. At best, only this thing will have survived. Everything else will simply have disappeared.'

Once more we sat in silence. I didn't say anything. I wasn't sure if I trusted myself to. I could feel the blackness in my nostrils. It was like inhaling tar. I found myself remembering a story I must have read as a child, about an old lady who sneezed and her whole body flew into pieces.

'I wonder . . .' said Rory.

'What?'

'I'm just wondering if we should move. We're not having much luck here, are we? What do you think?'

'If you like.'

The air felt sharper and colder when I stood up. Rory insisted that I keep his coat around my shoulders. We walked down to the water and made our way along another path. After a few hundred yards, it veered away from the river and through a farmyard. Then came a sharp left-hand bend. The path started to climb back up the bank. I could see Rory's cap bobbing about in front of me. There was sand underfoot now. My shoes slipped as the gradient grew steeper. Rory stopped and held a bramble out of my way.

As we began climbing up a long, shallow ditch, it occurred to me that this was almost certainly the same route used to haul the ship up from the river to the mound. Once, in this same ditch, hundreds of men had heaved and pushed. Moving the great ship from its natural home to a new, unfamiliar element. Hundreds of men, all feeling that another world lay just beyond their reach, perhaps just beneath their feet. I tried to imagine them now, materializing between the trees. Hauling on ropes and bending their backs. A distant clamour rising all round. Momentarily, they knotted before me, and then slipped away.

Rory turned his torch on again. We were close to the top of the ridge now. The ground reared into a kind of lip before starting to flatten out. I could see his tent, the guy ropes fanning out. There were some pots and pans outside the entrance, soaking in a bowl of water.

We continued on up the slope, emerging from the wood just by the shepherd's hut. Ahead of us lay the ship. Seeing it in the semi-darkness, approaching from an unfamiliar angle, I couldn't get over how raw it looked, how wanton. Pegged back like a giant wound. The wind had got up. I could hear the dry scratching of sand being blown across the tarpaulins.

Walking towards the mounds, I became aware of something dancing in the air. At first I thought it must be sand. But this didn't look like sand; it looked more like a cloud of snowflakes. As they fell to the ground, they caught what little light there was.

Rory had seen them too. He reached out his hand, palm upwards. Then he held it up to me. I could see something shining there.

'What is it?'

'I think it must be gold leaf. I remember Phillips saying how there was a lot of it lying around.'

The gold flakes continued to swirl about in the breeze. I could see them quite clearly now. I gazed in wonder,

watching the flakes settle on my shoulders and my chest.
Holding my hands out, I wanted as many of them to fall on
me as possible. I had this absurd fancy that I would be all
garlanded and crowned, like a princess.

But when I reached up to feel my hair, all I touched was
a piece of twig. It must have become caught there when I'd
been lying against the tree. I tried to disentangle it, except it
wouldn't come. I only succeeded in making it even more
tightly snagged.

'Here,' said Rory. 'Let me.'

I stayed still while he began unpicking the twig from my
hair. He did so very carefully, not tugging at all. Parting the
strands and then unwinding them. It was as if he was
picking me apart. All the while tiny specks of gold leaf
continued falling around us. I could feel them in my mouth,
catching in my throat. But still they were not enough to
stop this awful confessional urge that rose within me. It
seemed to gather up everything hidden, everything secret,
and carry it all out into the open.

'It's not what you think,' I said.

I felt Rory's fingers stop moving.

'What isn't?'

'It's not what you think,' I said again. 'With Stuart.'

'What do you mean?'

'Things between Stuart and me. They're not . . .'

'Sshh.'

I turned around. Rory was holding his finger up to his lips.

'Just listen,' he said.

I heard nothing, not at first. And then the birdsong came
from so close at hand that I almost jumped. There were
long gurgling trills, punctuated by a series of harsh little
clicks. Then the nightingale waited for a response. But there

was nothing, only silence. After a few minutes, the singing started up again, both louder and more passionate than before. Bubbles of sound streamed up into the night sky.

The sound was sadder than anything I had ever heard before. Full of yearning and desperation and the proximity of regret. The hope that drove the song forward seemed entwined with the knowledge that it would never be answered. Yet despite that I couldn't bear for it to end. I felt that as long as we stayed exactly where we were, then nothing need ever change. The earth would swallow us, just as it had done everything else. I wanted this more than anything.

But even then I knew it would never happen. I knew it before another torch beam cut through the darkness. It came towards us from the direction of the house. Behind the light, I could make out a black-clad figure.

'Good evening,' said a voice.

Neither of us spoke.

'My name is Police Constable Ling,' the voice continued. 'And this is my colleague, Police Constable Grimsey.'

Another man had appeared beside him. He was also dressed in a uniform and a flat cap.

'We have been asked to keep an eye on the site by the owner,' said the first policeman. 'In case of unauthorized visitors. May I have both your names please?'

I started laughing. At that moment, I felt an enormous sense of relief. Relief at not letting myself down, at not betraying everything that mattered to me. It was like a kind of exultation. I explained that I was one of the archaeologists working on the site and that Rory was Mrs Pretty's nephew. As I did so, I could hear the babble of my voice, the words tripping helplessly over one another.

'I see,' the policeman said when I had finished. 'In which case we won't disturb you any further.'

'In fact, I must be going,' I told him. 'I have an early start in the morning.'

'Let me walk you to your car,' said Rory.

'There's no need.'

'But it's no trouble.'

In silence we walked back towards the house. Rory kept the torch beam trained on the path in front of my feet. When we reached the car, he opened the door and waited until the motor had caught.

'Goodnight, then.' He was standing with his hand held up to his cap.

'Goodnight,' I said.

I awoke from a deep sleep to see a man's head hovering above mine. It was only a few inches away. As I gazed upwards, he bent forward and kissed me on the forehead. His breath smelled of Plasticine.

'Hello, darling.'

'What are you doing here?' I asked.

'I managed to catch the milk train. Sorry to wake you, but there have been developments.'

'What sort of developments?'

'Rather ominous developments, I'm afraid. The papers have got wind of everything.'

Stuart held up a newspaper. Slowly, the print unfurled before me. 'Anglo-Saxon Ship-Burial,' I read. 'Remarkable Find in East Anglia.'

'*The Times* has it as well,' he said, holding up another paper. This one was headlined, 'Sunken Boat is British Tutankhamun.'

'Phillips isn't in his room,' Stuart went on. 'I assume he has already gone over to the site. I've been trying to call Sutton Hoo House but there's no reply. Perhaps they're not up yet, although they should be by now, I would have thought. I think the best thing for us to do is head off there straight away.'

'May I have a few minutes to dress?'

'Of course, darling,' he said. 'How inconsiderate of me. Why don't I see you downstairs when you're ready?'

I stared through the windscreen as we drove along around the bottom of the estuary. Nothing had changed. Beyond Melton, the road still ran straight for several hundred yards. The petrified oaks still jutted up out of the mud flats. The fields of sedge grass stretched away on the left. There was a white mist lying over the river, through which I could hear the muffled cries of the gulls.

Nothing had changed when we drove into Sutton Hoo House either. We headed straight out to the mounds. Nobody was around. The tarpaulins were still fixed in place. I looked over at the woods beyond, but nothing stirred. We were about to turn round and go back when the two policemen I had seen the previous night emerged from the shepherd's hut. Neither of them made any sign of recognition. They had no information beyond the fact that Mr Brown had appeared first thing. Apparently he had sat on the top of the bank for a while, then gone away again.

Back at the house Grateley, the butler, answered the doorbell. Instead of lying flat, as usual, his hair rose in an oiled flap at the front. Mrs Pretty had left word that she was not to be disturbed. He said that journalists had started calling at seven o'clock that morning. After an hour of this, she had ordered that the telephone should be disconnected.

At that moment Phillips appeared in the corridor behind Grateley. Instead of being furious, as I had expected, he seemed to be brimming with bonhomie. 'Ah, Stuart,' he said. 'There you are. I assume you've heard what has happened. It's all Reid Moir's fault, of course. I should have known he wouldn't be able to keep his trap shut. No doubt he wants to make everything as awkward for us as possible. Well, if that's the way he wants to play it, let him do his worst . . .

'The BM thinks I should hold a press conference. Personally I'm all against it. Anything I say is bound to be distorted. Some idiot has already telephoned this morning and asked if the boat is still seaworthy. Mrs Pretty is understandably upset, poor lady. I have done my best to calm her, but she has gone back upstairs for the time being.'

'What do you think we should do about the actual dig?' asked Stuart.

'Nothing,' said Phillips promptly. 'We can't possibly continue in this sort of atmosphere. Not with all this nonsense going on. I gather there's a convoy of journalists on their way here now. The whole place will be crawling with them in a few hours' time. My intention is to let everything calm down for several days and then finish excavating the chamber. Assuming we're not at war, that is.'

'And what would you like us to do?'

'Ah, I've been thinking about that. Why don't you come back outside for a moment?'

Once there, Phillips lowered his voice – as much, it seemed, out of a love of subterfuge as anything else.

'Crawford has finally made contact and hopes to be here tomorrow. Plenderleith and Hutchinson have also offered to help. There's even a good chance that Munro will come. Under the circumstances, I thought you two might like to take this opportunity to slip away.'

'Slip away?' said Stuart.

'That's right. After all, you two are supposed to be on your honeymoon. I should go off and make the most of it while you still can. As I say, there isn't going to be much happening here for the next few days. I suspect we are probably close to the bottom of the chamber already. I doubt if there can be much more left to come. It's conceivable we may still find a body, although, as you know, I have always had my doubts on that score.'

'When were you thinking we might leave, CW?'

'No time like the present, is there? Not strictly true in archaeological terms, of course, but there's something to be said for it just the same. If you go now, you should escape all these wretched journalists.'

'What do you think, darling?' said Stuart. 'Darling . . .' he said again.

'I don't know.'

'I suppose we could just potter up the coast and take pot luck.'

'I assumed you would be keen on the idea,' said Phillips, sounding offended. 'Grateful even.'

'We are pleased, naturally we are. At the same time it's bound to be rather a wrench.'

'Yes, yes, but soon all this will be a happy memory. One to put alongside many others, I have no doubt.'

'Shouldn't we say goodbye first?'

'You can say goodbye. Right now.'

'Not to you, CW. I meant to the others.'

'As I mentioned earlier, Mrs Pretty is unavailable at the moment,' explained Phillips patiently. 'If you have any messages for anyone else, I will be only too happy to pass them on. Was there anything in particular you would like me to say? No? In which case I shall convey a general salutation from you both.'

'If you're really sure . . .'

'Perfectly sure.'

Phillips came across the gravel towards us, making shooing motions with his hands. 'Now, off with the pair of you before I change my mind.'

We drove back to the Bull. Stuart stayed downstairs while I went up to our room to pack. It didn't take long. After I had handed in the key, Stuart carried our suitcases and strapped them on to the back of the car. We made better progress than expected. By midday, we were already halfway to Norwich.

Edith Pretty
13–14 August 1939

All day Spooner and Jacobs trudge back and forth across
the lawn, emptying watering cans on the flower beds.
According to Spooner, the river level is so low that several
of the fishermen have begun anchoring their boats as far
down as Bardsey. At breakfast, to try to encourage some
semblance of a breeze, we have taken to opening the
windows wide, as well as the door. Yet it makes no
difference: the air just sits there, unstirrably thick.

Last night, a full-scale black-out exercise was held in
London. A report appeared in today's newspaper:

It was curious to see Piccadilly Circus, Coventry Street and
Leicester Square, which are normally blazing with lights until
well into the early hours, in more than semi-darkness. All-night
restaurants and cafés were open as usual. However, blinds
covered their windows and all bulbs had to be properly screened.
Inside, ghostly figures sat eating and drinking in a mysterious
half-light.

I put down the newspaper. Robert was still eating his
breakfast. The knife and fork no longer appeared so

unwieldy in his hands; he manages them now without any sign of awkwardness. I could tell that he knew I was watching him, but he would not look up. Instead, he lowered his head a little closer to the plate and carried on eating. He has been like this ever since the excavation ended. Doubtless he blames me for work having stopped. With no one to play with and nothing to distract him, his days pass in a brown study of frustration and inactivity.

'Robbie,' I said, 'how would you like to have your portrait painted?'

At this, he did look up in surprise. 'What for?'

'So that I can remember you as you are now.'

'Won't you be able to do that anyway?'

'Of course I will. But sometimes it helps to have a reminder.'

'What about a photograph?'

'A portrait is different from a photograph.'

'How is it different?'

'Because it has artistic worth. I have already spoken to a very nice man, a Mr Visser, who lives in Ipswich.'

'Could I wear what I wanted?'

'I would have thought so. Within reason.'

'Would I have to sit still for a long time?'

'I'm afraid you would. Although I am sure you could have regular breaks. Would you like that, Robbie?'

He thought about it and then said, 'I don't mind. If that's what you want. Please may I get down now, Mama?'

'Of course. If you are quite sure you have finished.'

After Grateley had cleared everything away, I went into the kitchen to see Mrs Lyons. There was a saucepan simmering on the range, its lid rattling, and some crescents of diced celery lying on the chopping board. The kitchen, however, was empty.

I found Mrs Lyons in the larder. She was sitting on a milking stool with the undersides of her arms resting on the tiled slab. On the back of her neck was a damp tea towel. She started to stand up as soon as she saw me and only sank back down after some persuading.

'I've been coming in here quite a lot recently, I'm afraid, ma'am. It's the coolest room in the house.'

It was indeed wonderfully cool; so cool I wished I could join her. Instead, we discussed arrangements for Thursday afternoon. We decided in the end that she should make two cakes – one with chocolate cream filling and the other with jam – as well as scones and brandy snaps. I was about to leave when she told me that Mr Trim, the butcher in Woodbridge, had had a change of heart and decided that he would be able to take our rabbits after all.

Afterwards, I went through into the sitting room. Grateley had closed the curtains to shut out the sunlight. At eleven o'clock, Spooner came to the back door. As it was my wedding anniversary, I had asked him to pick me a bunch of flowers. He was standing on the step holding a sorry-looking bunch of dahlias and pinks. Already they had started to wilt. Before I could say anything, Spooner started to apologize, explaining that these were the best he had been able to find.

During the afternoon, when the heat was a little less fierce, Lyons drove me to the churchyard. He waited outside while I lifted the latch and went through the gate. No one else was there. Dead stalks crackled underfoot. Everything was pale and washed out. Even the stones looked as if they had been bleached.

Frank's grave is unmarked, apart from a wooden cross. I have not bothered with a headstone as we are to be buried in a double plot. Placing the bunch of flowers by the foot of the cross, I stood there for a few minutes, asking for his guidance in what lay ahead. The sun was like a hand pressing against my back. I could see my shadow falling along the length of the grave. When I returned, Lyons was sitting in the car. He had his jacket undone and was fanning himself with his cap.

When I rang for Ellen on the following morning, she did not appear. I rang again. Still nothing happened. Eventually Grateley knocked on my bedroom door. Looking flustered, he said that he had not seen her since the previous evening.

'Do you think she might be unwell?'

'I cannot say, ma'am.'

'It is most unlike her not to send word.'

Grateley agreed that this was most unlike her and said that he would make inquiries. After I had finished dressing, I went down to breakfast. I was sitting there alone, still wondering what could have happened to Ellen, when Grateley came in again. This time he brought an envelope. He held it in front of him with his arms extended, as if he thought it might explode at any moment. My name was written in capital letters on the outside. I did not recognize the handwriting. Inside, was a single sheet of lined paper.

Dear Madam,

Please forgive me. I am afraid I am having to leave your employ with immediate effect due to personal reasons. I am very sorry to be leaving like this. However, circumstances

make it impossible for me to serve out my period of notice.
I hope only that you will not think too ill of me.
Yours truly
Ellen Spence

I folded the paper and put it back in the envelope. Grateley was still standing by the sideboard, waiting for a response.

'Thank you, Grateley,' I said. 'That will be all.'

On the way to the village hall in Sutton, we passed Mr Brown. I had offered him a lift earlier, but he insisted that he was quite happy going on his bicycle. He sat ramrod straight on the saddle with his pipe stuck between his teeth. Lyons sounded the horn as we went by. Mr Brown took one hand off the handlebars and lifted it in greeting.

There had been some dispute beforehand about the venue for the inquest. A number of people – Mr Reid Moir among them – argued that it should be held in the town hall in Woodbridge. However, the coroner, Mr Vuillamy, decided that the proximity of Sutton village hall overruled any concerns about its size. Matters were further complicated when, much to my dismay, the BBC announced that they intended to broadcast excerpts from the inquest on the National Programme. By then, though, it was too late for any change.

Beside the village hall a field of mangolds had been set aside for a car park. When we arrived people had already congregated outside. As I had expected, a number of press photographers were also there. Mercifully, none of them knew who I was. However, when poor Mr Vuillamy arrived a battery of flashbulbs exploded in his face. It was not until I saw him step back in surprise that I realized just how much I had been dreading this inquest – both because of the publicity it would bring and because of its expected outcome.

Inside the hall an oilcloth had been laid on top of the billiard table, with the tennis table placed on top of that – thereby making a serviceable if none too stable surface for the coroner and chief constable to sit behind. A jury of fourteen local men had been appointed beforehand. They comprised Mr Abbott, the Sutton village blacksmith, and his son, Percy, landlord of the Plough Inn; three farmers; two retired army officers; John Mann, the Melton grocer; Mr Peecock, the land agent; Mr Bett, the secretary of the Woodbridge Golf Club; the headmaster of the Sutton village school; Mr Houchell, a haulage contractor; Major Carruthers, the manager of the Midland Bank in Woodbridge; and General Charles Tanner.

Mr Vuillamy took his place behind the makeshift table with the chief constable on his left. The jury sat directly in front of him, with members of the public crammed into what available space there was behind. Those of us who were being called to give evidence sat at the side. A seat had been reserved for me between Mr Phillips and Mr Reid Moir.

The British Museum had sent a van containing several of the key finds, including the gold jewellery, the sceptre, a bronze stag and the great silver dish. These were displayed in a glass case provided by Mr Maynard. This case was guarded by PC Ling and PC Grimsey.

There were also a number of unfamiliar-looking men standing about. These, Mr Reid Moir informed me, were plain-clothed detectives, detailed to keep an eye out for any suspicious characters. When I asked him how he knew, he said he could tell by the cut of their suits.

The sun warmed the inside of the hut, releasing a strong smell of creosote. Mr Vuillamy began by giving a brief account of the excavation and the finds that it had yielded. The jury was then invited to inspect the display case, which they did, showing – in most instances – considerable interest in the contents. It took several attempts on Mr Vuillamy's part to make them sit down again.

The point at issue, he explained, was as follows: had the owner of the treasure been intending to come back to retrieve it at some point? If so, then the treasure would rightfully belong to the crown. Or had the intention been that it should accompany the owner on his journey from this world to the next? In which case it would belong to whoever owned the land it had been discovered on.

I was the first person to be called. In response to Mr Vuillamy's first question, I explained how I had spoken to the Suffolk historian Vincent Redstone at the Woodbridge Flower Show and mentioned my interest in excavating the tumuli. He had written to Mr Reid Moir at Ipswich Museum on my behalf. Mr Reid Moir then replied, recommending Mr Basil Brown.

'Had you had any grounds for believing the mounds might contain treasure, Mrs Pretty?'

I told him about the various myths and legends surrounding the mounds. I then added that I had always suspected there might be something inside.

'Can you explain what gave rise to such a suspicion?'

'Not specifically, no,' I said. 'It was merely a hunch.'

'A hunch,' repeated Mr Vuillamy, and wrote this down in his minutes.

Next, Mr Brown was asked for his account of events. He gave his testimony in a clear, strong voice, always leaving a gap of several seconds between the end of Mr Vuillamy's question and the start of his reply so as to make quite sure that he had understood everything properly before committing himself to an answer.

He was, he explained, a freelance archaeologist who had done work for Ipswich Museum on a number of occasions – most latterly at the Roman villa at Stanton. He went on to describe how I had engaged him to excavate the mounds and how, on 11 May, John Jacobs had discovered the first of the ship's rivets. A visit to the museum at Aldeburgh that afternoon had confirmed his suspicion that the rivet found was similar to several discovered in the Anglo-Saxon ship-burial at Snape.

During the early days of the excavation, he said, he had had the benefit of advice from Mr Maynard, the curator of Ipswich Museum. However, as the excavation proceeded and the dimensions of the ship exceeded all expectations, it had become necessary to call in outside help. This help had duly arrived in the shape of Mr Charles Phillips of Selwyn College, Cambridge.

After another pause, during which Mr Vuillamy consulted with the chief constable, Mr Brown was told that he could stand down. He was followed by Mr Phillips himself, who was asked to take up the story from the start of his involvement. He proceeded to do so, although on several occasions Mr Vuillamy had to ask him to speak 'in plain English' for the benefit of those persons present who did not have the benefit of his specialist knowledge.

Mr Vuillamy then asked why no body had been found in the grave. That, said Mr Phillips, was not an easy question to answer. There were a number of possible explanations, of which two stood out. The first was that this might be a memorial – a cenotaph – to mark the death of someone who had died elsewhere. Alternatively, the body might simply have been destroyed by acidity in the soil. Suffolk soil, he said, with a nod in the direction of Mr Brown, had an unusually high degree of acidity, especially in this area.

'You mean the body might simply have disappeared?' Mr Vuillamy asked.

'That is correct. Although such cases are admittedly unusual. Almost always there are some signs of a presence, however faint. Usually it is the teeth.'

These, he declared, were usually the last things to rot. Long after the bones had powdered away, the teeth would stay embedded in the earth, as hard as olive stones.

'How long do teeth take to rot?' Mr Vuillamy wanted to know.

'I cannot answer that question,' Mr Phillips replied. 'It would depend entirely on the composition of the soil.'

'Could you make an informed guess in this case?'

Mr Phillips regretted this was impossible. To do so, he said, would involve a degree of speculation incompatible with his professional expertise.

'I understand . . . And do you have any idea whose grave – or memorial – this might be?'

Yes, Mr Phillips said, he thought he did. The most likely candidate was King Raedwald, who was king of East Anglia from about AD 599 to his death in about 625. According to the Venerable Bede's *Ecclesiastical History of the English People*, Raedwald held sway over all the provinces south of the River Humber.

'Was King Raedwald a Christian?' he was asked.

That too was difficult to say, Mr Phillips told him. 'From the evidence of the treasure, he had both Christian and pagan loyalties. There are silver spoons and bowls with crosses upon them. However, there is also metalwork with pagan symbols on it, such as the gold and garnet jewellery with its interlaced birds and beasts.'

'So you could say that he was hedging his bets?' said Mr Vuillamy, to a burst of laughter.

'You could indeed,' Mr Phillips agreed. 'And by the same token, the objects discovered are a mixture of the official and the personal.'

'Could you explain that more clearly, please?'

Mr Phillips looked over the rows of attentive faces and sighed. 'By official, I mean that the dead man would be expected to fight on behalf of his people in the next world. As a result, there is a shield and a sceptre, as well as the remains of a helmet. As for personal objects, possibly placed there by a loved one, these include a washing bowl, shoes and various keepsakes, along with knives to trim his nails and beard.'

At this point the door opened to admit two late arrivals: Mr and Mrs Piggott. From the brief glimpse I had of her before she sat down, Mrs Piggott appeared to have lost weight, or perhaps she was just looking tired after her journey. No sooner had they settled themselves than Mr Piggott was called to give evidence. He was also asked about the lack of a body and confirmed that it was not unheard of for a body to disappear completely. He had personally come across a number of cases where this had happened.

'No teeth or anything?' asked Mr Vuillamy.

'Not even teeth,' Mr Piggott confirmed apologetically.

Due to the time – almost one o'clock – and the temperature, Mr Vuillamy suggested we break for luncheon. People sat about among the mangolds, chattering and picnicking. Mr Piggott stood beneath a tree, talking to Mr Brown, while Mrs Piggott went to stroke a horse which had hung its head over the fence.

I went and rested in the car. All this talk of decay, of obliteration, of any human imprint being swept away, had left me quite unfit for company. Of course, one could believe in the spirit surviving and not the flesh. As Mr Swithin had so often reminded me, different rules applied. At that moment, though, they seemed as fragile and impermanent as each other. Nothing endured, not in any sphere. There were no voices clamouring to be heard, no messages coming from some unimaginable beyond. That surely was the truth. Everything else was delusion. Crumbs of comfort to keep the pangs at bay.

People stared in curiously through the open window. Closing my eyes, I leaned back against the hot leather and willed them to go away. After an hour, everyone was summoned back to the village hall, where Mr Vuillamy summed up the evidence. Once he had done so, he told the jury that as far as he was concerned, there was no evidence to suggest the owner of the treasure intended to come back and retrieve it.

Although it was naturally difficult to attribute motives to people who were long dead, he cited, by way of legal precedent, the case of the *South Staffordshire Water Company* v. *Sharman* (1896). In this case the owner of the land – rather than the workmen who had made the discovery of a hoard of ancient coins – was deemed to have been the legal finder.

The jury was asked to retire to consider their verdict. Unfortunately, the only other room in the village hall was the gentlemen's lavatory. They made their way through the door in single file, accompanied by rather more laughter than before. Due to lack of space inside the lavatory, the chairman of the jurors asked if they might leave the door open.

Mr Vuillamy, however, decided he could not permit this in case anyone should overhear their discussions. By the same token, he ordered that the window should remain closed throughout. Everyone sat in silence, or conversed in low voices, while the jurors conducted their deliberations. I took this opportunity to ask Mr Brown, Mr Maynard, Mr Reid Moir, Mr Phillips and the Piggotts if they would care to come back to Sutton Hoo House for tea afterwards.

Twenty-five minutes later, the jurors re-emerged, in shirtsleeves now, with several of them mopping their brows with pocket handkerchiefs. A piece of paper was passed to Mr Vuillamy, who read it and once again consulted with the chief constable. He then tapped the microphone: the jury, Mr Vuillamy announced, had unanimously decided that the objects found were not treasure trove. As a result, Mrs Edith May Pretty of Sutton Hoo House was the rightful owner of everything that had been discovered.

The verdict hardly came as a surprise. After Mr Vuillamy's summing-up, the jury would have had to have been very obtuse to come to any other decision. None the less, everyone turned to stare at me in a direct, almost devouring manner. As I tried to leave, there was an unseemly scrum. The press of people on all sides almost lifted me off my feet. With Mr Reid Moir on one side and Mr Brown on the other, I was escorted back to the car. Lyons was standing there with the door already open.

We drove out of the mangold field and back on to the road. I should have felt delighted, of course. That was what everyone expected. But I did not. I felt no sense of abundance; I felt only lack. On the way home, I forced myself to concentrate on the view: this narrow strip of tarmac disappearing over the horizon, with fields of ripened barley on either side like an inappropriately parting sea.

Mr Reid Moir, Mr Maynard, Mr Phillips and the Piggotts arrived at the house a few minutes after I did. Mr Brown followed them on his bicycle. Everyone said how pleased they were for me – although not in Mr Phillips's or Mr Reid Moir's case with a great deal of conviction.

After that, a brittle sort of heartiness took over. At one stage, Reid Moir said how important it was that the finds should be properly displayed, by people who really cared for them and who had a connection with 'the locality' – but when no one took up this suggestion he fell silent. Nobody asked directly what I intended to do with the treasure.

Mr Brown seemed more relaxed than anyone else, possibly due to his being the only person present without a vested interest. He drank his tea with evident relish and when offered a second piece of cake wagged his finger reproachfully at Grateley as if he was being led into temptation.

When the heartiness gave out, Mr Piggott nursed the conversation along, talking about how unemployed men had been put to work digging trenches in London parks. Mr Phillips matched this with an anecdote about how his wine merchant had advised him to lay in extra cases of hock while stocks lasted.

Mr Reid Moir was evidently about to make a further

contribution of his own, but before he could do so Mr Maynard stole unexpectedly past him with a convoluted story about German soldiers climbing up the Virginia creeper on the outside of his house. This, however, turned out to be a recurrent nightmare suffered by his teenage daughter.

It was only after we had been talking for several more minutes that I realized Mrs Piggott was no longer in the room. I waited for a while for her to reappear and then, when she did not, went to see if she was all right.

She was standing by herself in the dining room. The curtains had been left half-open. A band of light, wide as a sheet, lay across the table, on which I had placed some photographs of the excavation taken by my nephew.

I spoke as much to alert her to my presence as anything else; I was not sure if she had heard me come in.

'There you are, my dear.'

Still she gave a start. 'I'm sorry, Mrs Pretty . . .'

'No, no. You stay where you are. I put out the photographs thinking that people might be interested and then they completely slipped my mind.'

Together we stood and looked at them. Broadly speaking, they fell into three categories: there were pictures of the ship itself, pictures of people at work on the excavation and pictures of the finds. Among the second category were four pictures of Robert and myself. We were sitting on top of the bank, looking down into the scooped-out interior of the ship. Robert was at my feet with his knees drawn up to his chin. I found it oddly disconcerting that he should be as motionless as I was.

'Is your son not here?' she asked.

'I have sent him away for a few days,' I told her. 'To the

south coast. I have some cousins there. I felt he needed a change. He has been a little downcast since you all left.'

There were also two pictures of Mrs Piggott. In both of them she had plainly been unaware that she was being photographed. In one, she appeared to have just straightened up. There were sandy patches on the knees of her overalls and her hair was in disarray. In the other photograph, she was staring at an object which had just been uncovered. The object itself was only partially visible – there was a dimpled section of metal in the bottom right-hand corner of the picture – but the expression on her face was clear enough. She looked awestruck as well as overjoyed, caught at that moment when her face was about to break into a smile.

'Sadly, my nephew is not here either,' I said. 'He had hoped to be, but in the end it was impossible.'

'Impossible?'

'Yes, it is simply too far from Aldershot. And I rather doubt if he would have been given permission.'

She stared at me, her face a confused tangle. 'I don't understand.'

'Rory has joined up – the Royal Engineers. I rather assumed you knew. He enlisted as soon as he left here.'

'No,' she said. 'No, I didn't know that.'

She leaned forward over the table. When her hair fell over her face, she made no move to push it away. Instead, she just let it hang there, like a screen.

'Would you like to sit down?' I asked.

She did not reply. After a moment or two, I took her elbow and steered her towards one of the dining-room chairs. Then I sat beside her. 'This heat is very draining, isn't it?' I said. 'Would you care for a glass of water?'

She shook her head.

'Is there anything else I can get you?'

'No . . . No, thank you . . .'

'Perhaps you would like to be alone?'

Again she shook her head, more adamantly this time.

'Why don't we just sit quietly for a while?'

Through the gap between the curtains, a corridor of brown grass stretched down to the estuary. Everything was as flat and devoid of colour as one of Rory's photographs. Mrs Piggott opened her handbag and took out a handkerchief. It had lilies of the valley embroidered around the border. For the first time I noticed that her hands looked more like a girl's than a young woman's.

As she sat staring into her lap, all at once it seemed very important that I should say something. It scarcely mattered what. Anything to stop her from giving way. I would not allow that to happen. Not to her, or to either of us.

'Have you both driven up here today?' I asked.

She looked up, her eyes full of tears.

'I have forgotten exactly where you and your husband live.'

'We live in a village . . . It's called Rockbourne,' she said, her voice tight with effort. 'About ten miles south of Salisbury.'

'Goodness, you have had a long journey. No wonder you are tired out.'

'We set off this morning. At four o'clock. But I'm afraid we were still late.'

'No need to worry about that. Tell me, my dear, do you have any plans now that all this is over?'

Her eyes met mine. There seemed something utterly bereft about her gaze. Yet I felt if I held it for long enough I might bear her up, might prevent her from falling.

'Stuart has been asked to do something by the university,' she said. 'Near Uffington in Berkshire. There's a large Bronze Age fort there.'

'And you will help him, of course.'

She nodded, then gave a flickering smile.

'He plainly depends on you a great deal.'

'Oh, I don't know about that,' she said.

'Do not doubt it, my dear. Not for a moment. You have such a fascinating life.'

'Do I?'

'Most certainly. Work like yours must offer such a sense of satisfaction.'

She did not look away. 'Yes . . .' she said, and lifted her chin slightly. 'Yes, it does.'

'And I am quite sure it will continue being a source of great joy to you. Joy as well as sustainment.'

Then I reached out and put my hand on top of hers. It cannot have been long afterwards that Charles Phillips's head appeared around the door. His eyes went back and forth several times from one of us to the other before he said, 'Ah . . . we were wondering what had happened to you.'

Basil Brown
August–September 1939

Reid Moir and Maynard have been going on at me all week to try to find out what Mrs Pretty intends to do with the treasure. I told them both – Reid Moir in particular – that I'd no idea what her plans were. I might have added that they weren't any of my business either. According to Maynard, Lord Churchman, the tobacco baron, has offered to build a special museum in Woodbridge to house everything in. That's assuming Mrs Pretty wants the treasure to be displayed in public. For all I know, she intends to put it back under Robert's bed.

In the days following the inquest, I had no chance to ask her about this, or anything else. She scarcely ever left the house. I thought that she'd want me to leave – after all, there was nothing left for me to do. But every time I mentioned this to Grateley, I received word back that Mrs Pretty would like me to stay for a while longer. That's assuming I had no objection.

I didn't have any objection, I told him. Part of me wanted to get home and see May, of course. Another part, though, needed the money. But that wasn't all. Something else kept me there. Despite everything that had happened, I couldn't bring myself to leave.

For two days I picked gooseberries in the fruit cages and then spent another two trimming round the game coverts. A couple of times Robert came out to see me, but he didn't stay long. I dare say I've rather lost my appeal since the excavation ended. For a couple of weeks there'd been talk of the Queen coming over from Sandringham to pay a visit. Apparently she'd been greatly interested in the finds. But in the event she had to cut short her stay and go back down to London.

One evening I came back to find out that the postman had left a parcel for me. Inside, I found five tins of my favourite pipe tobacco – MacBaren's Black Ambrosia. With them was a note that read:

Dear Basil Brown,
I hope this is the right blend. With many thanks and all best wishes,
C. W. Phillips

I was so surprised I even opened one of the tins to make sure there was something inside. My thoughts about Phillips had not been running along entirely Christian lines over the last few weeks. Yet for all that, I was touched by his generosity. I wrote back thanking him and saying how I hoped we might meet up again before too long.

Meanwhile, the weather had changed. Already the leaves were starting to turn. I told Grateley it was no longer safe to leave the ship open to the elements and asked him to find out what Mrs Pretty wanted me to do. Off he went once

221

again and came back saying that I was to protect the site as I saw fit. He also said that I was welcome to use Will and John again, but I told him I could manage on my own.

The simplest way to cover the ship was to lay strips of hessian on the lines of rivets, then fill the interior with branches and dry bracken. That should keep it reasonably well protected, at least for the time being. It should also ensure that it can't be seen from the air. On the top, I put a layer of conifer branches so that it wouldn't stand out. It worked far better than I'd expected. From 100 yards away, you'd never know there had been anything there.

Towards the end of the afternoon, I was coming out of Top Hat Wood, dragging a few last branches of larch behind me, when I saw Mrs Pretty standing by the shepherd's hut. At first I thought she was carrying her probing iron – for a moment it crossed my mind that she might want me to start excavating another mound. But as I came closer, I saw it was a walking stick.

After she had looked over what I'd done, she said, 'I could offer you a few more days' work here, Mr Brown. If it's of any interest. I wondered if you might help building an air-raid shelter. There are no cellars in the house and I fear the time has come when we need to take every possible precaution.' She paused and jabbed at the ground with the end of her stick. 'It will mean more digging, I'm afraid.'

I pretended to think about her proposal, although I didn't really need to think about it at all.

'Thank you, Mrs Pretty,' I said. 'I'd welcome that.'

It took Will Spooner and me three days to construct the shelter. We had to dig down ten feet, then sink a semicircle of corrugated iron in the hole. Once that had been done, the whole thing had to be covered in two feet of earth and topped off with turf. By the time we had finished, it looked like we'd buried an elephant.

All that time I never read a paper or listened to the news. And we didn't talk much either when we were working, not about anything important anyway. But for all that I seemed to know just what was going on in the world. Everyone did. There was no escaping it.

On the morning of the second day, Will came in and said, 'The prime minister is addressing the nation at eleven o'clock. That can't be good, can it?'

'No,' I said. 'I wouldn't have thought it could.'

'Mrs Pretty says we can all go in and listen to the wireless in the kitchen.'

'I don't think I will, thanks.'

'You sure, Baz?'

'You go,' I told him. 'I'll stay here.'

At ten to eleven, Will went inside. I carried on inside the air-raid shelter. We'd brought a paraffin lantern so we could see. A ventilation pipe had already been fixed on to the roof, but still the flame guttered and burned blue. The work was simple enough – just a matter of laying planks on a wooden frame and banging in a few nails. But at least it kept me from dwelling on things too much. Even so, I couldn't help remembering being told how I wasn't fit to fight last time. How far it had knocked me back. And there was another thought I couldn't swat away – about how this was the only chamber I'd actually been allowed to set foot inside.

Will wasn't gone long – twenty minutes at most. When he came back in, the light from the paraffin lamp sent his shadow leaping up the curve of the wall. He didn't say anything. He just looked at me and nodded. Then he picked up his hammer and started banging away.

On the following day – and the day after that – German planes flew over Woodbridge. They circled around several times before heading off north, up the coast. Both times Billy, Vera and me reported for duty at the Air Raid Warden's post at Bromeswell. As no uniforms had arrived yet, there was a good deal of confusion about who was in charge. Various busybodies bustled about, telling people what to do, but no one paid them any attention. Instead, everybody sat round swopping scare stories. As soon as the all clear sounded, we came straight back again.

That afternoon Will and me finished the shelter. When it was done I went back once again to Grateley to ask what I should do now. But this time he didn't have to go and find out. He already knew.

'Mrs Pretty said to tell you that there's no longer any reason for you to hang around, Basil. She suggests you spend the rest of today packing your things and come round tomorrow at nine o'clock. She'd like a word before you go.'

'Right,' I said. 'I'll do that, then.'

I'd accumulated quite a bit more stuff than I'd arrived with – there were the clothes that May had brought, as well as my notes, and Maynard's book in Norwegian – but Billy said he was coming over to Rickinghall next week and could drop my case off then.

At five to nine the next morning I wheeled my bike across the gravel and rang the bell. Leaves quite stiff and dry spun towards me on the breeze. Grateley answered and asked me to wait. Mrs Pretty wasn't long in coming. She walked slowly down the white-tiled corridor, stick in hand.

'No doubt you will be relieved to be going home, Mr Brown,' she said when she had reached the doorstep. 'And I am sure that your wife will be delighted to have you back.'

'I hope so,' I said.

It was only now that I saw she had an envelope in her spare hand. She held it out towards me. 'I would like you to have this, Mr Brown. As a token of my appreciation.'

'Mrs Pretty –'

'No,' she said, 'It's the very least I can do. And there is something I wanted to tell you. It seems only fitting that you should be the first to know. After giving the matter a great deal of thought, I have decided to give the treasure to the British Museum. I know how much this will disappoint Mr Reid Moir and Mr Maynard, but I believe a find of this importance should be seen in a national collection. I also thought you should know that I have written to Mr Phillips, telling him that I expect your work to receive proper recognition in any written account of the excavation.'

When I'd thanked her, I asked if Robert was around – I'd hoped to be able to say goodbye to him. But Mrs Pretty said that he'd left the previous evening to start his new school in Ipswich.

'Perhaps you'd remember me to him.'

'Of course. I know how sorry he will be to have missed you.'

After that we shook hands. Then I tucked the envelope inside my jacket, swung my leg over the crossbar and cycled off down the drive. Beyond Rendlesham, they were burning stubble. The columns of smoke were visible from miles away. Around the edges of the fields avenues had been ploughed to stop the flames from spreading. Even so, a number of hedgerows had already caught fire.

Everything crackled as the wood and dry stalks burned. Along with the smell of the burning stubble, there was a deeper, darker smell of charred earth. Partridges rose wildly into the air, screeching as their nests were consumed. Rabbits and hares, terrified by the flames, ran across the road. But they were only escaping from one inferno into another. The whole landscape was ablaze. There was no longer any sign of the sun.

Ahead of me, the road rose and disappeared into a bank of grey smoke. As I rode towards it along the ash-covered tarmac, my wheels made no sound at all.

Epilogue
Robert Pretty
1965

For many years I did not return to Sutton Hoo. It was not a matter of deliberately staying away; there was just no reason for me to go. After my mother's death in 1942, I was sent to Lymington on the south coast to be raised by her cousins. But although Sutton Hoo House had been sold after my mother's death, I still retained, through deed of covenant, the rights to excavate the site.

Last autumn, I was approached with a request. The British Museum wished to reopen the mound the following summer and see if anything had been missed the first time around. They also hoped to compile a survey of the whole group of barrows. Would I give my permission for such a project? This I willingly agreed to do and work began at the beginning of May.

However, various commitments kept me from visiting until the end of June. Rather than drive up to Suffolk, I decided to take the train to Melton and walk the rest of the way. After leaving the station, I crossed Wilford Bridge, then turned right along the sandy track that runs through the woods. On the right, water meadows shelved down to the river's edge. On the left woods rose up the bank.

I'd almost reached the estuary when it struck me that I hadn't given a moment's thought to the route I was following – this despite my not having been here for almost twenty-five years. Seeing Sutton Hoo House on the bluff above me, I started to climb through the trees. As I did so, I had a strange sense of something missing. For a while I couldn't put my finger on what it was. Then I realized there were no longer any rabbits around. They had all disappeared, presumably because of myxomatosis.

As I approached the mounds, I saw that a great shelter had been erected – a corrugated-iron roof held in place by a mass of struts and scaffolding. Beneath it, the ship had been exposed once more. My first impression was how different it looked to the way I remembered. Instead of lying more or less flat in the ground, the ship now had a twisted, even agonized appearance.

This was due to a number of factors, I was told. During the early days of the war, the army had taken over the grounds of Sutton Hoo House for use as a training ground. Slit trenches had been cut in several of the mounds, while others had been used as targets for mortar practice. Later on, Sherman tanks had left deep tracks all over the site.

To make matters even worse, the ship had been left unprotected – apart from a layer of branches and a few pieces of sacking. The gunwales had disintegrated, along with the upper strakes. Rather than attempt to preserve what was left, the decision had been taken – reluctantly – to dig through the crust of sand to see if anything was buried beneath.

But first a plaster of Paris impression was being taken of the whole site. For a while I watched as white blocks of plaster were winched out of the hull on a block and tackle.

Then one of the archaeologists asked if I would like to see their most recent discovery. He took me to a freshly dug pit about fifty yards from the stern of the ship.

There, in the bottom of the pit, I was astonished to see a body. It was lying on its side with its legs bent and its arms resting on its knees. The body was the same colour as the sand – completely brown. Over the centuries, I learned, it had literally turned into sand. As the organic matter had decayed, so it had been replaced by what lay around. What was being defined was the shape of the flesh itself.

Yet while the outline of the body had survived, there was, in effect, nothing there. Nothing except a thin crust of sand. Inside the crust, there was no sign of a skeleton; there was just more sand. Any attempt to remove it was sure to make it crumble away in an instant. All the archaeologists could do was take samples and measurements, then fill in the grave again.

Time had blurred the body's features into anonymity and had almost made it melt into the earth. For all that, though, it hadn't succeeded in destroying it, not entirely. Something, if only a fragile shell, was left. At that moment, as I stared down into the pit, this felt like a consolation of sorts.

When I asked if they had any clues to the body's identity, I was told that no grave goods had been found. Judging by the extent of the decay, it almost certainly dated from around the time of the ship-burial. But that was as far as anyone could go. Everything else was guesswork.

At lunchtime, we sat on the grass by Top Hat Wood, eating sandwiches and passing around photographs that had been taken during the 1939 excavation. Among them was a photograph of my mother. She was sitting in a wicker chair with a blanket draped over her knees, peering down into the ship. Her head was turned away from the camera and only a pale wedge of chin could be seen beneath the brim of her hat.

The archaeologists turned out to know a lot more than I did about what had happened to everyone – or almost everyone – involved in the original dig. I was delighted to hear that Mr Brown, now in his late seventies, was still in good health. He and his wife had been over several times to see the site. Despite having injured his leg in a fall, Charles Phillips had also visited and had made a number of suggestions about how the work should be conducted. Mr Reid Moir, it seemed, had died some years earlier. As to what had happened to his deputy, Mr Maynard, that remained a mystery.

Mrs Piggott had lived in Sicily for a number of years, following her divorce. There, she had married a Sicilian, but sadly this marriage had also failed. Recently, she had moved back to England and was understood to be working on the first of a projected two-volume study of Roman beads. As for Stuart Piggott, he was now Professor of Archaeology at Edinburgh University.

Nobody, however, knew the identity of the photographer. I was able to tell them that the pictures had been taken by my cousin, Rory Lomax, who had been killed in 1947, when the motorcycle he was riding collided with a lorry.

As I was leaving, another of the archaeologists said that they had been sifting through the original spoil heaps when they had found something they thought might belong to me. He went away and came back carrying an old shoebox. Inside was a rusted piece of metal with what appeared to be four wheels attached, one at each corner. Only after I had removed it from the box did I realize what it was: a single steel roller-skate. It sits on my desk now as I write this.

Robert Pretty
October 1965

Author's Note

This novel is based on events that took place at Sutton Hoo in Suffolk in the summer of 1939. Certain changes have been made for dramatic effect. I would like to thank the following people for their help: Robert Erskine, Ray Sutcliffe, Angela Care Evans, Rosalind Cattanach, Peter Geekie, Sue Annear and Jane Eldridge. I'm especially grateful to Martin Carver, Professor of Archaeology at the University of York and Director of Research at Sutton Hoo, for taking the time to read the manuscript. Any mistakes, of course, are entirely my own.

He just wanted a decent book to read ...

Not too much to ask, is it? It was in 1935 when Allen Lane, Managing Director of Bodley Head Publishers, stood on a platform at Exeter railway station looking for something good to read on his journey back to London. His choice was limited to popular magazines and poor-quality paperbacks – the same choice faced every day by the vast majority of readers, few of whom could afford hardbacks. Lane's disappointment and subsequent anger at the range of books generally available led him to found a company – and change the world.

'We believed in the existence in this country of a vast reading public for intelligent books at a low price, and staked everything on it'
Sir Allen Lane, 1902–1970, founder of Penguin Books

The quality paperback had arrived – and not just in bookshops. Lane was adamant that his Penguins should appear in chain stores and tobacconists, and should cost no more than a packet of cigarettes.

Reading habits (and cigarette prices) have changed since 1935, but Penguin still believes in publishing the best books for everybody to enjoy. We still believe that good design costs no more than bad design, and we still believe that quality books published passionately and responsibly make the world a better place.

So wherever you see the little bird – whether it's on a piece of prize-winning literary fiction or a celebrity autobiography, political tour de force or historical masterpiece, a serial-killer thriller, reference book, world classic or a piece of pure escapism – you can bet that it represents the very best that the genre has to offer.

Whatever you like to read – trust Penguin.

read more
www.penguin.co.uk